The Painter's Friend

Also by Howard Cunnell

Fathers & Sons

The Sea on Fire

Marine Boy

HOWARD CUNNELL

The Painter's Friend

PICADOR

First published 2021 by Picador
an imprint of Pan Macmillan
The Smithson, 6 Briset Street, London EC1M 5NR
EU representative: Macmillan Publishers Ireland Limited,
Mallard Lodge, Lansdowne Village, Dublin 4
Associated companies throughout the world
www.panmacmillan.com

ISBN 978-1-5290-3092-1

1 3 5 7 9 8 6 4 2

A CIP catalogue record for this book is available from the British Library.

Printed and bound by CPI Group (UK) Ltd, Croydon, CR0 4YY

Visit **www.picador.com** to read more about all our books
and to buy them. You will also find features, author interviews and
news of any author events, and you can sign up for e-newsletters
so that you're always first to hear about our new releases.

for John Healy

I was in earnest always or I was nothing

John Clare,
John Clare By Himself

The Painter's Friend

She doesn't run, Mrs Whitehead said. You can't go anywhere.

Late October, maybe November. Hadn't kept track.

Evelyn Crow once said I had invented the idea of myself as an outcast but here I was. Leaving the city. Doors locked behind me. Ghosting through the picture-loaded streets, past a man out cold in a doorway. Cardboard sign illuminated apple yellow. The sign so closely packed with text I couldn't read a word. A long story. Nobody to read it but himself.

The bare bulbs of the market stalls lit the fruit in bonfire colours. Meat on hooks was heavy ruby stillness, white borders. A corn-coloured dog appeared from the darkness under a wooden barrow. The dog held a lettuce leaf in its mouth, and the green shimmered against the faded black of the barrow's painted wheels.

Businesses boarded up, except for the pawnbrokers and bookies, the legal highs and tattoo places, and junk shops selling the past. The stuff desperate people sold for food money or their dead left behind. Suits worn to a shine, broken-down shoes, old uniforms, service medals, rings of beaten gold.

The Spitfire pub stood at the end of a row of gutted houses. Pale men half seen moving in and out of the dark spaces inside.

The heavy pack's canvas straps cut into my shoulders and the sweat was wet on my back.

Stopped at a hoarding. The wide barrier stood in front of what used to be a skatepark and was now a building site, for flats no one living round there now could afford. The hoarding was collaged with graffiti, carvings, tribute band posters, a missing person flyer.

Gill, a pretty girl with a shiny face. Ribbons in her hair. Sunday clothes. Missing. She might have been fifteen in the photo. The picture was old. She wouldn't look like that any more.

A repeated pattern framed the girl's picture, made from stylized hearts and what looked like a bird with its head turned backwards and something, a pearl maybe, in its mouth.

Ran my hand over the hoarding, bumpy and hard with the thick glue paste that covered it, a dimly reflective surface in which moving traffic, people, me, were hinted at in muted and fleeting colours.

Got knocked into, sworn at, forced to move along.

A barefoot man with dark matted hair and a rope for a belt said:

Go and come back.

Sky the colour of wet concrete.

What you're doing, Crow had said the first time we talked, looking through my drawings, pencil and felt tip, charcoal, crayons, my paintings on hardboard and used canvas, might have some purchase.

Tall, angular, dressed in black. Scent of fig and mint from his freshly shaved head. Glasses with blood-red frames, behind which dark eyes were sharp and clear. Snowy skin that looked cold to touch. Holding a drawing to the light. Humming. A man looking at a treasure map and trying to decide if it's the real thing. Charcoal study of ex-miners on a beach in Kent. Crow smiled at me. The drawing trembled, held between the thumb and forefinger of his right hand. Knotty wrist, stones under the skin.

I knew who he was.

Crow had made a ton of money for Burke Damis, whose huge, larger than life paintings sold for the kind of money that makes the news, and were shown in the best galleries, though not lately. Hyperreal, they called his work. I thought it was flash. A one-trick horse with a castle in California. Vineyards. Damis had produced no new work in years, but thanks to his assistants the stuff kept being churned out. After Ariel Galton, who had once been married to Damis, drowned herself at sea, Crow became her biographer with Burke's approval. Together the two men made another fortune from the handful of abstract paintings Galton had left behind. Ariel Galton was my mentor, though we never met, let alone spoke.

Human fallout, Crow said, still looking at my work. I like it. There might be a window.

Voice like honey. Loving Crow's voice was one of a thousand regrets that made the roaring in my head.

Tell me there's a painting of this, he'd said.

The miners. Six men grown old. Black suits thin as paper. Shoes with worn heels. Hadn't worked since the strike.

Blacklisted. Thirty years. More. Rolled cigarettes no thicker than matches.

In the drawing four men were making a ring for two of their companions who were about to fight. A deserted car park overlooking a beach in Kent. The squared, imagined ring, its dimensions and limits, seemed summoned from shared memory. Understood by the men standing like knife edges at its corner points. The barechested old fighters even seemed to lean against ropes that weren't there. The beach, the grey corduroy sea and banked sky, going on forever.

The landscape dominates, Crow said, but I can't help thinking about these men. You have to really look to see them. Who are they?

I told him.

What happens to people like that? Crow said.

Crow promised me my first big painting show. All new pictures. Worked for two years solid, thinking about nothing else. Last chance. Be sixty in a year, making pictures for most of that time. Still burned for them to say I was good. Crow said I was. Promised to make it happen. Let myself dream about the red-tiled, whitewashed house in the sun I'd finally be able to buy, with a terrace framed by hibiscus, stone steps leading down to the Mediterranean. In the shade of the flowered arbour, a young woman with a long brown throat places fresh wine on the sun-worn table.

Picasso in old age was said to give young women he wanted to get to know figurines made of solid gold – a likeness of the artist with a great big whanger. All I wanted for

4

the rest of my life was to look at light patterns moving on endless blue water.

The money didn't come through. Suspected Crow of lining his own pockets. Fixing the prices low without telling me. Using proxy buyers. Getting my work cheap.

They said I attacked him with a tyre iron or a large kitchen knife or both. Armed with a machete. Crow said he'd been too terrified to remember, but that I'd definitely had a weapon. Crow said: Knowing Terry's past, I was in fear of my life.

It's true I threatened to kill him but I was unarmed.

I'd been homeless, locked up and even sectioned. On my own since I was a kid. Who were they going to believe, me or the powerful gallerist, who once confessed to me his surprise he'd not been knighted?

The word went out. Don't buy or show his paintings. Don't reply to his texts. Don't take his calls or answer the door. Don't let him in. I couldn't get near them.

If my name was ever mentioned in public, it was always associated with violence.

Crow said he had supported me for two years, and that sales of my work had not even covered his expenses.

The unsold paintings were given to Crow for costs and damages I could never hope to pay. The experience of painting had been one of happy work. Filled with the light I was making.

I'd taken many photos but the images had none of the power they once had in my mind.

—

Went back to work on the rollers and brushes. A building site is a place of constant piss-taking, but I was lower than a beaten dog. My co-workers left me alone on my painter's scaffold. From up there you'd hear a hundred things worse than anything I was supposed to have said to Evelyn Crow. You'd hear laughter, too.

But the work dried up and soon I was on the out again. Read about the boat on the noticeboard of the artists' studio where I was sleeping on the floor unknown to anybody.

Needed to move fast or I was gone.

When I said I wanted to rent the boat for a year the owner jumped at it.

She just sits there in the winter ordinarily, Mrs Whitehead said, and of course we're out of the country by then. Without somebody to pump the bilges and light a fire her condition deteriorates terribly.

Promised not to dump my shit in the river but always use the cesspit, and the boat was mine. So long as the mooring fee was paid by direct debit every month. I hoped to last the year, but if I was too free and easy with the money I'd saved I'd have no chance.

She doesn't run, Mrs Whitehead said. You can't go anywhere.

The sky became a sweeping wash of tangerine and coral pink. Infills of deep purple that would soon dominate. A fairground sky.

Night beat me to the river. From out of the darkness I could see the falling mid-air whiteness my directions had said to head towards. River water falling over the weir that led to and from the island. Beyond this whiteness was a darker, high mass that was the forest of ash trees that gave the island its name.

The iron weir crossed over high and fast running water. Lights were studded in the pilings, the illumination they gave off flaring up at me so that I made the crossing in a dense white glare, with the deafening sound of water I couldn't see falling all around. I felt my way across the walkway, freezing spray hitting my face, my boots clanging on the iron.

At last I stepped onto the island, into the restored and quiet dark. Didn't have a torch though I was told to bring one in the neat, handwritten note that was sent with the keys.

There are a few paths, Mrs Whitehead had written, but mostly the ground is rough, overgrown, and there are many exposed tree roots you can twist an ankle on or worse. There are no medical services.

She had said the moorings would be ahead of me as I left the weir. Hidden by the trees whose presence deepened the darkness I walked in, and whose top branches I could hear high above me on the river wind, making their shell-to-the-ear sounds. Rising up around me was the thick smell of wet soil.

The boats were in lines of three, and by chance my boat was in the front rank, nearest the riverbank.

A woman stood in the bow of what looked like a barge somewhere towards the back of the line, wrapped in perfumed smoke from a held bundle of incense sticks. Visible breath a mark of early winter. Face and hands white against a dark, too-large overcoat worn draped over the shoulders like huge wings. Cropped head. A penitent figure who could or who could not be said to be looking for patterns in the river, but who might just as well be watching other patterns on the screen of mind.

Thin columns of woodsmoke showed above several boats. There were lights showing, and like the smoke that told of fires, or the absence that didn't, when lights showed or went out here would always mean something. Somebody new is coming. A big man with a bigger pack, moving slowly, heavy boots.

A converted lifeboat from a retired White Star liner, Mrs Whitehead had explained, with a large wheelhouse grafted on to her. All planes and curved surfaces of wood and glass. Crossed the gangplank and stepped on deck and the boat pushed away and pushed back under my boots.

Found the light switch in the wheelhouse and the

suddenly visible river around the boat, the island bank on my near side, the starboard side of the boat next to mine, the interior of the glassed-in wheelhouse, all became golden and navy-edged.

At waist height next to the wheel and control panel were makeshift plywood double doors, padlocked, that opened to steps down into the living quarters. There I found a small galley, a two-ring gas cooker. A jar of instant coffee, enough for a couple of cups, no other supplies. A settee covered with a worn red blanket. Gas lamps were mounted on the bulkhead. A stove. Small pile of cut wood.

The dampness in everything was a quality of thickness in the air. I stopped noticing it after a minute. The bow was behind a hand-sewn patterned quilt that functioned as a curtain, where a bed made thick by blankets and other covers took up all the space.

Every movement produced another beneath me.

Everything was squared away, Mrs Whitehead calling in a favour, or paying somebody. Coffee was a bonus I hadn't expected, and I set about making some.

No drink, I said to the loud voice inside my head. You're not having any.

Didn't stop me searching the boat to make sure there wasn't a bottle on board.

In time I made a smoking fire. Ate the food – bread and cheese – I'd brought with me. Lit the gas lamps and turned them down low. Didn't know how much gas I had. Took a cover from the bed and wrapped it around me, looking into the fire and trying to become used to the lack of solid ground beneath me. The cabin became a moving space of varying and competing patterns of light and dark, as though I was being held in the process of submersion, and at any moment would continue my descent.

Next day I went walking with my drawing book to better understand where I was.

To the south, a few hundred yards downstream, was a three-arched bridge faced with rose-pink brick and what I believe was Portland stone.

Not a reinforced bridge carrying the recognizable forms of cars and vans and lorries towards the city, but a sequence of shining ovals both in and out of the water, while above these forms sometimes passed at irregular intervals an indecisive pattern of stalled or moving coloured marks.

Found a chest-high pile of large stones crowned with yellow leaves. The top stone was heavy, smooth to touch and patterned in marine shades of grey and white. It was not of the forest. The stone and its companions looked like stones you might find at the bottom of the river, and I thought they must have been gathered from the island foreshore at low tide and brought to this place. Not all at once but over a period of years.

This was in a clearing from where a number of rough paths radiated. I wondered if the stones were a marker, though no direction was indicated or, as far as I could tell, needed on so small an island.

Michael was written in scuffed and faded black marker on the big bottom stone. I wondered who Michael was, and if what I was looking at was his work, as nearby I found groups of leaves that seemed recently to have been made into patterns: coronas, thick fans and huge circles all made from leaves of varied brightness.

Almost tripped over the wreckage of a Mariner four-stroke engine abandoned in the forest. Everything was slick and wet. As Mrs Whitehead had warned me there were tree roots everywhere. I wondered about wild animals. Twice I heard what I thought was a shotgun. Crows rising from the trees each time.

A deflated orange football sat on a plain wooden picnic table that was almost submerged by lichen. A small dinghy filled with water tied alongside a boat so consumed by mould it looked derelict. Flat-tyred bikes under dirty tarps among the trees. Burst sandbags. A blue water butt on its side. Ropes in great quantity lined the riverbank, coiled or hung from tree branches. A cat's cradle of weathered ropes held the bankside boats to found or made moorings. Scaffolding poles thick with rust and warped planks were jury-rigged to make gangways to the boats.

Sound travelled a great distance. The soft hollowed-out scoop of a paddle making a cut through the water. I could hear the drops of water falling from the blade to the river in soft sequence, but in the velvet light of early morning the canoe with its single pilot was only a dark, drifting smudge.

I would not dump my shit into the river. I would keep to myself, and keep a tight lid on my anger.

Though I believed I could turn some of them into a healing tea, I did not collect the red winter berries that grew along the riverbank for fear that they would poison me.

Next day I walked into the boatyard store with mud on my boots. The sandy-haired man behind the wooden counter looked at me with no expression on his face. Mouth a straight hard slash. Dirty blue eyes. Some scar tissue. Fair eyelashes almost transparent in the muted light that came through the small, high windows. Thick smooth hands. Clean-shaved, the skin on his fair cheek inflamed, sensitive. Close-fitting blue shirt. Wax jacket. Not tall, but he filled his clothes with hard edges.

The floor swept as clean as it could be.

Scraper outside, the man said.

Missed it. Sorry.

Didn't need an enemy. Went back out and stamped and scraped my dirty boots as best I could, jamming my bare hands under my armpits. Wet and freezing. Getting dark.

Three crows sat on the chain-link fence surrounding the yard. When one hopped sideways the others followed, keeping the same distance between them. Blue and orange gas bottles stood in ranks, shining wet with rain.

The sandy-haired man hadn't moved. No heating except for the blower I could hear behind the counter.

Help you?

The boatyard and store were on the other side of the island from the moorings, the same side as the broad-crested weir and lock that linked and separated the island to and from the mainland.

The weir meant that the water level at the moorings was several feet lower than the boatyard side. The river also had a significant tidal reach. At low tide my boat seemed almost to scrape along the bottom, and everything on the island seemed high up and far away. At high tide we rose on the brimming river, almost level with its banks.

Part of the store was given over to a chandlery, for trade with the owners of whatever moving boats called on the island.

Tins of food face out so that their labels showed. Tomatoes, sardines, ravioli, beans, soup. I picked out a minestrone. The label of the tin behind was face out, in line. Jar of Nescafé. Same. The bread tray was empty. Have to come earlier. Have to come back with a list. Work out a budget. Down here things were limited. Things, including money, would run out.

Sign on the door: no credit.

Liquorice papers?

What I'd come in for though it was a long shot.

He had tobacco back there and a box of different papers. The last of the smokers. No customs stamps. Couple of boxes of shotgun shells next to the tobacco.

I wondered if the shots I'd heard in the forest came from his gun.

Something of the fighter or ex-mercenary about him. Saw him crouched on a contested airstrip, cool under small-arms fire.

How many?

I'll take three packets.

Paid for the papers and the soup. When I opened the door, and the thundering sound of the water was once more amplified, he was coming around from behind the counter with a floor brush in his hand. An economy of movement, like a man once confined to a small space with other men.

I held the door open for an angry-looking man with a shaved head, and huge eyes so dark and unlighted they appeared black.

The woman with him was younger and taller, with short hair and a very upright posture, as though she were carrying with care something I couldn't see. She wore a red cotton thread around her wrist. Like me, both of them had thick mud over their boots and up to their knees.

Neither of them had used the scraper, but the hard-edged man didn't correct them as he had me. In fact he seemed happy to see the woman.

Perseis, he said, hello again. And Gene.

The angry man glared at the storekeeper but either he didn't notice or he didn't care. He was still looking at the woman, who wore the same long black coat as my late night water watcher, and I was sure it was the woman I had seen.

She turned and looked at me with eyes so deeply blue they were nearly violet.

I wonder if we might borrow Anthony for a moment? she said.

I was just leaving, I said.

In the yard a red phone box. I had a phone, an ancient

Nokia, but signal on the island was unreliable, especially at the moorings. I'd put the Nokia in a drawer and almost never thought about it.

Tied to the little jetty was a big gleaming boat. The water was thick with fallen leaves, and the broken whiteness of the boat's reflection.

The high fence around the yard was locked in the sandy-haired man's absence. When it was locked you couldn't buy gas. No gas meant no cooking, no hot water and only a battery lamp or candle for light.

It was bad enough for just a couple of days but I bet there were people who went without gas for weeks at a time until money was found from somewhere. Black winter nights, rain in pools on the partly frozen, umber-coloured ground, and points of candlelight in the black shapes of windows softly rising and falling as the barge rocked gently in the freezing water.

Kids came running into the yard, dirty-faced, whooping and shouting, carrying home-made bows and arrows and wearing oversize jumpers and boots, parakeet and crow feathers in their long hair.

A boy, older, maybe twelve or thirteen by his height, wore a wolf mask, the thick rubber kind that you wear like a balaclava. The kids all screamed when they saw me, a monster to run away from. When they screamed there came back from a place unknown to me a rattling volley of barking, a woman's voice calling the kids home.

The couple came away from the boatyard. In the falling

light the woman's face was so clear I thought I might see my reflection in it if I ever got close enough.

The man lifted the gas canister onto his shoulder. A tremor rippled over his body in a continuous wave and then stopped. He stood up straight.

I hate that geezer, the man said, he's a posh cunt.

The woman with the rare violet eyes didn't answer, but raised her head and looked up at the huge sky that was almost all black dark now, starless but stars would come, with the last traces of light disappearing in the west.

Thump thump thump across my deck. My outside neigh-bour going ashore. An old man in warmer looking clothes than any I'd brought with me. Lives on a narrowboat, talks to himself. Loudly. Breath visible. Seen that kind of reefer coat in old war films. Up periscope. The fast white lines of torpedoes. The destroyer sunk. Survivors into the lifeboat. Desperate men adrift.

The coat is navy, double-breasted. Thick as a blanket. Looks ancient, stiff enough to stand by itself. Wide collar turned up so that under his dark wool hat I couldn't see much of the old man's face. Dark canvas trousers, ancient shin-high sea boots. Bloody thumping over my deck first thing. Boat sinking and rising with his weight. Old man so he goes slowly, but he doesn't hesitate or hold on. A beaten track long before I got here. Thump and then waiting for what feels like forever for the next. Thump. Like a diver. Bottom of the sea. Lead boots.

There's nobody living on the barge between us, which is under a black canvas that collects rain and is sometimes plastered with ash leaves and bird shit.

Winter cold. A fight to get warm in the morning. To crawl out from under all the blankets and piled clothes and relight my fire. Waking dreams. Evelyn Crow at the point of my gun. My fist. Am a great painter. Everybody says so.

But Crow won't tell me where my paintings are. Despite his broken teeth, the blood on his suit. So I hit him again. And again.

Thump, thump.

Though often it's the smell of freshly ground coffee drifting across the river air from the old man's narrowboat that wakes me before first light. Strong enough to cut through the solid planking of my boat and into my head. Fall for it every time. I am a rich and famous painter. In a white bed in a high white room with French windows open to my blue sea. A distant white sail. The windows framed by sweet and vivid roses. Downstairs my fair but suntanned young lover, wearing my gift of a gold necklace, is making coffee. I fall back asleep knowing she'll wake me.

Thump. Thump.

Useless hard-on and no coffee.

The disused engine is down there, beneath my neighbour's boots. Stilled machinery and trapped dead air. A lot of hollow space. The boom of boots on deck reverberates across the still river. Birds should rise in alarm from the trees, but I'm the only one it seems to bother.

The bitter cabin air is almost visible in flavoured waves. Cold woodsmoke edged with damp. Just enough left of the coffee smell to piss me off.

Put more clothes over the ones I slept in. The stove still warm if I'm lucky. Embers. Bank it up quick. Make a Nescafé still wrapped in blankets. Smoke a roll-up. A good morning. When I have gas and tobacco and firewood and enough instant in the jar.

The canvas wrapping the barge between us is only some-times thick with leaves and bird shit because after heavy winds or a period of rain the old man climbs up and clears the leaves and shit and water.

A goat on a rock. Not falling off. Deliberate movements. Steady. Got a brush with a taped handle. Ridiculous. Time he's finished he's got to start again.

The old man of course takes pains about clearing his own narrowboat of leaves and bird shit, but he clears the empty boat before his own, most of which is also winter-ized with a protective canvas covering.

The exposed cabin doors and stern are detailed in strong colours: red white and blue with orange decking. There are painted roses and a castle on the cabin doors and, especially during the worst of the black winter days, the painted stern is often the only source of brightness I can see. Makes me wonder what the rest of the boat looks like under the tarp. Likewise the old man's thick outer garments protect him from examination.

If he owns both boats that would make him king of the island. Am I supposed to clean my boat? If it's some kind of rule everybody else is ignoring it.

Each morning involves an appraisal of conditions as I build a new fire. Supplies. Money. Weather. State of river, light, mind. Voices in the head – the drunk who lives inside trying to trick me into making a mistake.

Then the old man comes thumping across the inside of my head.

A pirate with two wooden legs.

Slowly the boat warms and the cabin air blurs and smokes once more. I like to go up to the wheelhouse with my Nescafé and roll up. Begin a new drawing. Looking up from my work at some fast movement outside – too late to see a bird passing, or the reflection of a bird passing on glass or water. Cormorants, kingfishers and a single grey heron hunt on the river undisturbed.

Rare tugs pull barges stacked with freight.

Across the river were a number of large white houses, with big gardens leading down to private jetties. The river, the unknown quantity of all that cold water, made the houses further away than they looked – about half as far away as the bridge downstream. Whichever direction the powerful river currents were travelling, you'd have to navigate them to make the other side. There was no straight line across. It was against the far bank of the river in front of these houses, a soft-edged stretch between river and sky, forest green and brown and gold, fringed with willows, that I once saw the outline of a police launch patrolling the jetties and little inlets.

If the old man hasn't crossed before I get up there he'll see me in the wheelhouse when he does. Cloth bag under his arm that looks stuffed with papers. Talking to himself. So I have to wait for him to cross my boat before going up to the wheelhouse.

Standing completely still in the gloomy cabin with the plywood doors to the wheelhouse closed. Gulls flying up the river in heavy traffic. The boat creaking against the fenders. Waiting means I'm not free so I could easily come to hate the old bastard. Despite the fire some part of me was cold all the time.

I think he wants to talk.

Looked into the wheelhouse and saw me.

Coming back late. Wherever he'd been had knocked the stuffing out of him. Crept back with no noise. Looked cold and wet. Sore with age. Stiff coat holding him up. A full shade darker it was so thick with rain. Keeping tight hold of his bag. You'd almost say he was smaller than before. Seen through the light of my lamp, the water-streaked window, the night and the rain. Face of hard planes and angles.

No sounds but the rain beating on the roof of my boat. A man seen through a series of obscuring lenses. Relieved only by low and patchy light, the waxing moon. Couldn't see the colour of his eyes, only that they were not clear.

Seen through the gaslight.

Wavering and yellow.

Tired. Long day.

But you didn't look like that when you left.

Like a drunk pulled up by the cops and fighting to look sober.

I blanked him and was pleased with myself. Turned away until I heard him slowly crossing over the empty boat between us. Soon as he left I drew him. An apparition.

Stomp across my bloody boat every morning and see where it gets you.

The boat's empty because nobody wants to live next to him. That was the obvious explanation.

Man owned the other boat or he was a lunatic, abroad at

all hours, climbing over boats like a robber on the rooftops of a sleeping town.

Giving me no peace.

Had to find out.

Next time I needed supplies I'd ask the sandy-haired man.

Had to wait my turn. A couple in puffa jackets wet with rain, and dirty trainers, loaded groceries onto a wheelbarrow. Sacks of rice and flour. Packs of water, tinned food. Bulk buying. Smart because cheaper.

The man wheeled the barrow out.

I held the door open.

Who is my neighbour?

Blue eyes went somewhere else, came back to me. Hesitated. I asked him for tobacco. Put it next to the small pile of other things I was buying. Watched him make up his mind.

What he told me didn't have to be the truth.

John Rose, he said.

And was he a sailor?

A merchant seaman. When he was young. A machinist for donkey's years. Factory closed. Redundancy. Here ever since.

The storekeeper looked at his dirty floor and grunted. Wiped the counter clean of something only he could see.

What should I know about him? I said.

The old man's wife died, he said. Leave him alone.

Rain streamed down the big wheelhouse window. I couldn't see much beyond the stern. Some debris being rushed downstream. I wasn't going outside. My fire was lit and I had a cup of coffee. I made and smoked a liquorice paper roll-up.

From my supplies I had brought out a sheet of butcher's paper, and I was drawing mushrooms I'd collected in the forest. Later I planned to make a mushroom tea with honey. See if anything happened haha. The butcher's paper held the line of a sharp pencil really well.

First smoke makes you need a shit. Finding the portaloo full, I swore. Should have done this yesterday. Lifted the bowl from the container, and finding the cap behind the toilet I screwed it on. Strong temptation to empty the shit into the river.

Then again the sound of a couple of gallons of piss and shit going into the water would be unmistakeable. When I rented the boat Mrs Whitehead had told me it was sanctioned practice to push the offender in after his shit if you caught him at it.

Carried the heavy container up the steps to the wheelhouse and out into the rain. Carefully. Rain fell on the water, drummed on the ground and the container, and against the waterproof that covered my head and body, making the material crackle. Downstream the bridge was made invisible by the weather. Every boat that could had a fire lit, but the tang of woodsmoke barely cut through the rain.

From the west of the island I heard the faint, complaining sound of an electric sander or angle grinder. I walked on the towpath towards the forest, falling rain visible against the dark treeline. Past a barge I hadn't noticed before.

A fair woman was emptying the contents of the bucket she carried into the river. She was wearing a gabardine raincoat dark with rain, and what looked like bright gypsy trousers tucked into an old looking pair of black boots.

When she saw me looking I didn't say anything, though I may have grunted a little when I shifted the shit container to my other hand, the contents sloshing around inside.

The ash tree canopy protected me from the worst of the rain and softened the noise of its falling. Towards the cesspit the forest became dark. There was grey wet light at the edges of my vision.

The opening of the cesspit was covered in stained planks. I kick-flipped the boards clear and stepped back. Thousands of flies droned below. The rain dampened down the worst of the stink, but I could still taste shit at the back of my throat. I placed the container horizontally on the slippery boards so that the sealed top was over the opening, and leaning over the pit, I unscrewed the cap. I raised the base of the container and turned my head as the contents began to empty and fall loudly into the wet pit. As was always the case I felt some splashback on my hand. I washed my hands and rinsed out the container at the standpipe.

When I came out of the forest the woman in the raincoat was still emptying the bucket over the side of her boat. Dirty water, it looked like. The kid with the wolf mask was carrying a saucepan by the handle with both hands. Looking hard at the pan, his tongue sticking out between his teeth. The woman paused to look at me with grey eyes, wiping the rain from her face. Long tied-up hair the colour of wet straw. I placed her in her early thirties. Somebody who loved her might call her pretty, but the woman would have a hard time believing it. Red half-moons of pinched skin under her eyes. The gabardine was not waterproof. The kid walked in slow motion across the wet deck, balancing the full saucepan.

Shit run? the woman said.

Shit run, I said, raising my empty container.

The kid emptied his saucepan and raised it at me. Rain made a hard pinging noise against the steel pan.

I went aboard my boat. Left my waterproof and boots in the wheelhouse. The need to shit had come on strong again. I fitted the container to the seat and filled the flushing mechanism with water.

Afterwards, I went up to the wheelhouse and got back into my wet things, swearing.

At the barge the woman was holding a squeegee mop over the side, using the lever on the mop to wring out water. There was a long and tall grey dog standing motionless on

26

the bow in the rain, watching me. I stood my ground, unsure around dogs. I couldn't see the wolf kid.

What's the problem?

Water in the hold, she said.

Need a hand?

I showed her the bucket I'd taken from the shower stall.

You're OK, she said, thanks. It happens. We've got it.

Sure?

She looked up at me, clear-eyed, standing with her feet apart on the deck, holding the mop by her side.

Sure, she said.

Danny, she called to the invisible kid, time to go. Get your bag, your lunch.

Every morning the kids crossed the weir to a waiting school bus.

Leave the mask behind, the woman said.

The dogs barking and howling in the night had to be monstrous. Huge-headed and scarred. Straining at thick chains sunk into heavy concrete blocks, and snapping their jaws at anything that came near. Ground littered with old shit and bones. Their cries dragged me out of my dreams of revenge and glory. I didn't know where the dogs were and that made it worse.

They live in the forest, the woman on the barge, Stella, had told me.

Wild dogs?

There's a camp.

Not your dog?

Joins in sometimes. Gets excited.

Right. And the people?

Yes, she said, there's people up there.

What kind of dogs are they?

Mongrels?

The kind that look friendly and then bite you, I said, or the kind that just bite you straight away?

I went up on deck, listening to the dogs. The ash trees were bowed in the wind and rain. It would be hard living up there.

I'd lived outside. From when I was a kid. Wandered

through England, sleeping in empty houses and parks, other people's fields, falling in with the ravers and travellers, free movement and free festivals, a loved-up kid drawing by a fire, waking in the smoky blue dawn to riot cops charging the camp, breaking heads and kicking over blackened pots and dirty mattresses. Locked up again, fighting, taken from prison to the nuthouse because they don't know what to do with you, sectioned, a blue rubber mattress and enough Thorazine to knock you out for years, the unit shut down, cuts, released to shuffle through identical sodium-lit shopping centres in different towns, spending what gets thrown at you on knockout drugs and drink that tastes flammable as you suck it down. A bloated lump of meat in a filthy sleeping bag, pissed-on cardboard boxes, an easy target for the lagered-up steroid boys, you don't feel the kicks until the security guard moves you on at first light, standing well back because you stink so bad you shit yourself you cunt?

Everywhere I went men smoked outside pubs where it was always happy hour, or stood in the street clutching plastic bags never full enough of tins of strong lager, looking like they wanted to fight the daylight.

Years. Finally stopped fighting and drugging. Put a heavy lock on my anger. Into the squatting scene. Started making art again.

Scavenged materials. Paintings and drawings of the world around me. Worked as a painter on building sites to support myself. Years of that. Jack's as good as his master. Work hard. Drug-free.

Put on a couple of small shows. In a squatter's cafe. A room above a pub. Local reputation. I even sold a few. Not expensive. Mate's rates or in exchange.

Evelyn Crow was the person I'd given up believing would ever come.

Fig and mint soap like a brand. Dark suit always with a darker, nearly invisible stripe. Somewhere there had been a reinvention, he'd polished himself up. Could play the kiss or the stiletto. An open wallet, a fixer. A key. I never thought of him as a friend. Smart though. Went along with him, because I believed he would take me to the sun country at last.

I've talked to Burke about you, he said.

Looked around, cleared the chair of drawings and paper. Took a white handkerchief from his inside pocket and wiped the seat and the arms of the chair. The small piece of cotton blazingly bright.

Burke Damis? I'd said. I thought he was living in a castle in California?

A chateau, Crow said. Let me just say, when I first met Burke he was living in a place not much different to this.

I fucking doubt it, I said.

Two rooms above a boarded-up and empty cafe. The head of a crossroads. Heavy traffic. For sale sign had been up for eighteen months. Bars on the windows. Metal fire escape up to my door. I could hear anybody coming.

My rooms were unfurnished except for the chair Crow sat in, and a mattress on the floor. My pictures covered the walls. The wood floor was splashed with paint. I tried to keep at bay the film of grime that covered everything else. The mantelpiece was a decoration of no fire.

Had enough of shared houses, squats, that's what I told myself. Past fifty. But more than one person had made it clear that I was considered difficult if not impossible to live with.

There was a small window in the bedroom, facing the south. I worked in there.

The moment is coming for marginal art, Crow said.

Kept quiet. Looked at him. Lot riding.

Crow looked at my drawing books and pictures for a long time.

Clearly you're not ready for a real show, he said at last. But work hard for a year, eighteen months, and you might be.

A year?

Maybe two.

The young, ambitious and famously poor Burke Damis had once been Ariel Galton's assistant. Crow's book said a vision sent Galton to the south, below the downs and near a river. There she built basic structures to live and work in. She lived alone except for Damis, who turned up unannounced at her door.

Seven years later, Damis and Ariel Galton, who was twenty years older, married before leaving on a long-planned trip to Colombia, where Ariel's voices had told her she must go. The couple disappeared into South America for eighteen months. They were separated within a year of their return. Galton's mental illness the reason given. We never heard Ariel's story, not least why she finally walked into the sea. Whatever she had to say was in her work.

The series of paintings Damis began after the separation, *Burke and Ariel in Barranquilla* (1993–94), became wildly successful, and made both Damis and Crow, his dealer, famous.

The best known painting was a huge canvas of Galton after she had been given electroconvulsive treatments in the hospital in Barranquilla, where she was kept for a month after Damis had committed her.

They never divorced, and after Galton killed herself by swimming out to sea, her home and paintings went to Damis. He bought the land and buildings outright, and preserved her studio. Damis also asked Evelyn Crow to be his dead wife's biographer.

Between them the two men owned quite a few of Galton's most important pictures. Crow's book established her as a great, forgotten artist. Galton's remaining works were sold to private collectors. Damis had later fronted a popular programme about modern art. Never got shown now because all the artists were white men.

I come from southern working people who value privacy above their own well-being. A problem shared is a secret given away. Whatever stories were told among ourselves were never written down, and nobody else thought we were worth writing about.

That's why I don't know why Nan was bringing me up in the first place, or why my mum, who I did not see, was unable to. What series of bad events had brought me to Nan's door. She never told me. Nan was expert at using silence against loss and absence.

My dad was never spoken of. Didn't stop me thinking about him.

I could draw for as long as I can remember. Everybody except Nan tried to kick it out of me, when I was a kid, but it was who I was.

The few people who bothered told me to learn a trade. Something more realistic.

Say the word Nan and you think of an old lady but she was younger than I am now when she died.

Clearing out her things I found a small black and white photograph with *Terry, 6 months* written on the back. A baby sitting on a blanket on a shingle beach, staring out to the sea that even in this colourless picture dances with points of light. Nothing has changed.

Hard to remember what she looked like. Dark and small like many southern women. Hooped earrings of flattened gold. Cigarette voice. Hard hands. Kind kind kind. Lost to the heroin that flooded the town, arriving with northern gangs whose own towns had been lost to shipyard, pit and factory closures. When she went into the fire on a cold May day Nan weighed less than four stone. What I remember is her arm across my chest, lightly holding me still while she talked to a younger man also with gold earrings who may have been her dealer, or who could have been just about anyone else. I push against the loving bar of her arm but she holds me in place.

After she was gone I took off. Nobody could have stopped me and nobody tried. Not the man with gold earrings or anybody else. A sixteen-year-old runaway.

I'd go along all right for a month or half a year but then the sky would fall in and I'd wake up behind a locked door. Cold bars on the window. How bad it was depended on whether I was strapped down.

The summer when I was twenty-one. Walking to a strawberry farm where I'd heard I might get work as a picker. I was covering the south of the country this way. I got lost somehow, turned around. At a white gate to a small private road, I saw a sign for an exhibition of paintings by somebody I'd never heard of.

I walked up the private road that curved towards the house. Expecting any moment to be stopped. There was that sweet suspension of the air you sometimes get on early summer days. I can't remember if the road was lined with flowers, just this droning sweetness that made me forget my sore feet in boots, my hunger. But it was England in the summer so there must have been flowers.

A small display of drawings. Some letters, a notebook full of columns of numbers. A large black and white photograph. Ariel, side on, is climbing a stepladder. Long hair thickly plaited. She holds onto the ladder frame with her left hand, in her right she carries a large level, or maybe a two by four with an edge she trusts. Wearing what looks like a quilted Chinese jacket. A palette knife and a decorator's brush are sticking out from the pocket. She's looking beyond the photograph. Smiling.

The paintings were in another room. There were four of them. The first floated in its frame and stopped me. I carried everything I owned on my back. I took the pack off and put it on the floor and then I sat on the pack and looked at the painting. Maybe ten feet tall and twenty feet wide. No human or animal forms. Bands of muted but reverberating colour arranged in a pattern, handmade, vulnerable, a grid made by visible pencil marks. Grey or grey-white paint, pale at the edges of each band almost to the point of absence. Ariel said that the pattern of a painting, the dimensions of the grid, was preordained in visions. The quilted squares of her jacket made another grid, and I wondered if she was conscious of that.

The process, she wrote, was like waiting for and then writing down the characters for a language she did not understand but was trying to learn. Hard work and practice as much as inspiration. She destroyed paintings she decided were failures.

I couldn't say where the house was, or who it belonged to. Near Chiddingly maybe. Somewhere on the downs. It's the feeling that remains. There was a show of her work in New York a few years ago but how was I going to get to New York? I can always make the floating grids appear.

I have visions too. The loving bar of Nan's arm. Bars of cold iron and radiant paint. My angels in the trees.

—

Crow was looking out at the unexceptional street. Checking to see if his car was still there. There were kids on the corner. They had nowhere else to go, but I guess Crow saw trouble. The hats and hoodies. A young woman I hadn't seen before jogged down the street, her buttery ponytail bobbing. The kids watched her pass. A dog barked once and then stopped.

A few days before, a skip had appeared outside the cafe downstairs. Two young blokes had pulled down the boards and begun stripping the place out. It was only a matter of time.

What did Damis say about me? I said.

Picturing the two men by a blue pool. Behind them the floating American hills. Hibiscus petals on the moving surface of the water like flowers of blood.

Damis had exaggerated his youthful poverty. Traded on it. Not been on the street or anywhere near it. Hitched around Europe with a guitar and a paintbrush. Getting loved-up by the senoritas.

Burke's not had it all his own way, Crow said. Recent reassessments have been critical. The representations of the Wayuu tribespeople in the Colombia series are now seen as problematic. But he's in good spirits.

I should bloody hope so, I said.

Burke said to tell you to listen to me.

I can't afford to work for another year on your say so or his.

Crow reached inside his suit again. Came out with a thick roll of money in an elastic band.

Keep using this cheap paint, he said, it's got an interesting quality. These abstract pictures look recent. They don't convince. Knock it off and stick to working these up.

Crow handed me a pile of loose drawings, and sketchbooks with pages marked.

The dogs began barking again as the wind seemed to pick up off the river. Like someone they didn't know was wandering around out there. Invaders. Dogs bark when they want to tell you something.

I stood in the dark, listening to the dogs and thinking about Evelyn Crow and Burke Damis. Ariel Galton and Michael's stones and the camp in the woods. I thought about the old man thumping across my deck. I'd put on my bed every blanket I could find. Cold despite the fire that still burned in the cabin. I hoped they had shelter up there.

You'd want a generator, or some way to cut into the island's power source. Each winter worse than the last. Nobody on your back though. No guards or cops. What else was there? The red berries that might or might not be poisonous. Different kinds of mushrooms. Whoever was up there would need to know a lot more than I did. Useful to know how to forage. Never learned. Knew what to do in the city, where the big waste containers can provide food and shelter.

Maybe they had friends on the boats. Get a hot shower, charge your phone. I imagined small raiding parties going into the city.

I liked the way the shape of Michael's stones remained unchanged despite the bad weather, but at the same time they were always different to look at. Dark with rain, or collaged with blown debris from the forest floor.

I heard the helicopter coming up the river from a long way away.

Cops. Searchlights from the thundering machine flooded the boat. Held its position directly above me. The boat rocked violently on the disturbed water. I held on to the frame of the wheelhouse. As the helicopter finally passed over the moorings, and the storm of its progress lessened to a kind of deep churn that made me bite down to keep from shouting, I watched with other dark heads now appearing from open hatches. The old man's star-rimmed outline, Stella, her arms around the boy, the dark figures of the couple I'd seen at the boatyard and had not seen since. The helicopter, port and starboard lights red and green, hovered over the treetops, stripping the last of the leaves and making the branches whip back and forth, its searchlight on full beam and raking, no doubt, through the camp in the forest.

I knew they could always decide it was you they were looking for.

When it finally went away all the dogs on the island continued the wild and furious barking they had begun before the helicopter came into sight or reach of human ears, and which had been drowned out by the deep thumping noise of the machine's rotating blades.

The kind of sunless, freezing day when the sky seems to finish just above your eyeline and the top of your head feels heavy. I'd been without gas for three days and had come up to the boatyard hoping to find the place open, determined to get in the yard somehow and take one of the bottles if it wasn't.

Finding the place open for business I exchanged bottles with the sandy-haired man.

I bought some instant coffee, four tins of beans, the kind with sausages in them, and two tins of potatoes. Some bread that wasn't quite fresh but it would do for toast. More tobacco and liquorice papers and two tins of sardines. I ignored the plastic litre bottles of wine. He wanted a pound for a chocolate bar and I wouldn't pay it. Paid for everything and put it all in the canvas bag I'd brought with me. The man didn't offer to help. He was looking at the paper he had open on the counter. The paper was the wrong way round, but I could see he was reading the sports page. A small picture of two upside-down boxers going at it.

Two kids in muddy boots tramped across the churned-up ground outside the hut. Nearly teenagers if they weren't already. Mucking about. I'm a golden one and my name is Goldie, one called to the other. I'm a golden one and my name is Goldie. They were marching across the yard in a game but I couldn't work out the rules. You could see the breath of the girl who was talking.

The other was wearing a rubber wolf's mask. Danny. I think there were about eight kids living on the boats. More at the weekends.

Danny smiled and waved at me and I was so surprised I waved back.

I hoisted the gas bottle onto my shoulder. Danny and the other kid ran off.

The man followed me out into the yard. He was doing up his wax jacket.

What are you doing here?

Buying gas, I said. Which I had to wait three days to do.

You're Terry Godden.

I looked past him.

You're not going to cause any trouble.

I took a breath and looked at him.

Rain fell between us.

What kind of trouble?

The kind you were in before.

I didn't answer. Stayed where I was. Couldn't just walk away from him.

Would you have gone through with it? he said.

With what?

Killing that man, the gallery owner.

I have two large Galtons, Crow had said. At the house in France. Remarkable power. The vision thing sells. The mad shaman. More true to say she worked hard, and the harder she worked the more visions she had. She was fighting her illness all the time.

I hadn't seen Crow for weeks.

Private club. In town. Crow known by name of course. I'd come straight from work. Show about to open. Finishing touches that would ruin the picture if I wasn't careful.

Should have put that in the book, I said.

The wine was sweet. I drank some more.

Took hold of my knife and fork and made them do the cancan along the edge of the table. Thick white linen. Doing the music. Somewhere else. Visions of sea light honeycombing before my eyes.

We're going to have to move to a smaller space, Crow said.

What? I said.

The interest isn't as high as I'd expect it to be by now, Crow said.

To use the big gallery will eat into any money we might make.

Terry, he said, we should lower the prices.

Terry, are you all right?

I burned with an ancient hatred.

You robbing bastard, I said, you fucking cunt.

I looked at the sandy-haired man. Anthony, the woman had called him. It was cold in the yard and both of us were trying not to show it.

I told him I'd cut his head off if I found out he was steal-ing from me, I said. It was a figure of speech.

I don't see the difference.

Neither could he.

So you wouldn't have killed him.

Last time I looked he was still alive, I said, and making money.

Christmas Eve I got drunk on the mainland and fell down into the boat late at night. The tide had changed. The boat was low in the water and in the dark I didn't account for the greater drop. Was pissed. Eight or nine feet but to me the fall lasted forever. I lay under a surface covering of mist that made the night silver and into which the river and the electrical cables and the trees had disappeared.

Don't know how long I lay there. It was very late or very early.

Standing over me when I woke up was a blonde giant whose green eyes shone out from his battered face. Wondered where I was, in the half moment before I felt the boat moving beneath me and tasted the dampness edged with river funk. The sheepskin-lined canvas jacket I wore saved me from broken bones and freezing to death.

The giant was just a kid.

When he spoke he almost disappeared behind his visible breath.

Lucky, he said.

Fuck happened.

Had a fucking skinful mate. Recognize the signs.

You're too young to have a face like that.

You hit your head? he said.

A big busted nose and scarred eyebrows that shelved out

above those shining green eyes. A full beard put years on him. A voice I couldn't place any more accurately than West.

A black wool hat. Gaffer tape covering the maker's name on his waterproof jacket. Boots. Huge and thick. Woodsmoke, sweat and cooking grease.

Fucking freezing, he said. Can you walk?

In an out of the fog of his breath went his face.

Did I piss myself?

You'd know better than me.

More or less had to carry me. The steps down from the wheelhouse to the cabin were too narrow for both of us. He went first in case he needed to break my fall. He was so big he had to go down sideways.

The cabin was cold and damp and was smaller with him in it. The cold closed air was smoky with all the fires I'd made that winter. He helped me lie down on the broken-springed settee in front of the burned-down fire.

Want me to take your boots off?

No, I said. The lamps though.

He lit the gas lamps, and a pattern of lighted bars and shadows appeared on the floor and walls. I looked at my hands. No blood.

The giant banked up the almost dead fire. There was a tin of lighter fuel by the stove and he whooshed some of that on and the flames rose.

Grit crunched under his boots as he moved around the boat.

He seemed to duck down reflexively, as though he was used to everywhere being too small for him.

You'll be all right now I reckon.

Moving closer to the fire. My wet clothes began to steam.

I reached into my coat pocket. The bottle was unbroken.

There's rum, I said.

I don't drink, he said.

Where did you come from?

The outsized youth gestured towards the forest.

He was looking at the worktable heaped with drawings.

Not just a piss artist then.

Look, I said, I appreciate the help.

But fuck off, right? I get it. You got your bottle stashed away. Have a nice drink in peace. I'd get out of those wet clothes before you start though. Catch your death.

Not like that.

Adam, he said. Merry Christmas.

When he left the boat lifted in the water, without the weight of him holding it down. After a long time I managed to get up and padlock the doors to the cabin steps and turn off the gas lamps. Then I sat in darkness broken only by the diminishing light of my fire, breathing hard.

Christmas morning he was sitting against the wheelhouse wrapped in a big sheet of dark green tarpaulin he'd found from somewhere. I barely made it up the stairs from the cabin to the wheelhouse. I was holding onto the doorframe. Even in the cold I was sweating. At the same time the rain was freezing against my face. I was foul smelling. Everything hurt. I tried to stand up straight. My back felt broken.

Rain drummed against the boat, and made endless expanding circles appear and disappear on the surface of the river. There was a narrow lip where the roof of the wheelhouse extended out, and a band of dryness on the deck under the lip, maybe two or three inches, and as far as he could, which wasn't much, he was sitting in what shelter this offered, with his back against the curved white exterior wall of the wheelhouse. His back would have been dry but the rest of him, even wearing the tarpaulin like he was, would be soaked through. His heavy-looking boots, wet and shiny now, were stuck out in the rain on the dark planking of the stern. I guess he would have got tired of trying to sit cross-legged for the difference it made.

The day was lead-coloured mostly, with a dull silver band showing in the sky above the arched bridge of Portland stone, and the far riverbank, what I could see of it, looking further away in the rain than it was. The big youth seemed to be looking at the traffic of floating things that were carried downstream without pause on the always moving water. A branch with a plastic bag caught on it. A jaunty-looking piece of white polystyrene. He turned to look at me when the wheelhouse door slid open, his fair beard dripping and sticking out from a gap in the tarpaulin, green eyes shining.

Had a dry bag with him.

I can't have anybody here, I said. I don't. I'm not.

The giant pushed himself up from his inadequate shelter. As he moved, rainwater ran from the folds and channels of the tarpaulin.

You just turn up, I said.

Lucky for you. Be dead otherwise.

Adam, you said.

That's right.

And you live in the camp.

What I said.

I stood blocking the doorway.

Let me out the rain at least, he said.

I stood aside.

A zephyr of fresh coffee. I looked across to the old man's boat and saw him through the blurred porthole watching us over the lip of his cup.

Adam was reaching into his dry bag and putting things on the corner of the banquette. I watched the rainwater make a little pool around his feet.

There was a dirty towel on the floor, just inside the door.

Use this? he said.

I nodded.

He used the towel to wipe the surface water off himself, and then rubbed his face and hair. Balled the towel and dropped it where it had been.

You can't stay here, I said.

He looked at me.

Painkillers, he said, shaking the plastic container so the pills rattled. Strong. Four a day. Don't fuck about or they'll fuck you. Plus, I didn't know what you had, so I got you some things, see you through for a few days.

A jar of coffee, tins of soup and beans. Corned beef. Bread. A tin of peaches. A thick battered paperback book. Burke Damis on the cover, dark hair swept back, sparkle in his eyes. *Modern Art*, the book of his TV series. With colour plates. Must have been thirty years old.

Where did you find this?

I'll be back in a day or two, he said. You all right for gas and firewood?

I said I was.

You'll need money, I said. For all this.

Sort it out later.

Threw me a roll of toilet paper.

Almost forgot, he said.

What kind of pills? I said.

The good ones.

I can't take them.

They're really good.

I looked at his broken face.

I know, I said. I can't.

Adam looked at me hard and nodded.

Going to hurt to wipe your own arse, he said. When the drink wears off.

Yes.

Get you something else?

No.

If you change your mind, he said.

All right, I said.

Merry Christmas.

And to you.

I sat in the wheelhouse after he left. The unopened book on the banquette seat beside me. The rain slowed almost to nothing. The wideness of the river slowly revealed in the early morning. The water tiger-striped in light and shadow, its surface now an endless series of moving helices. A diving cormorant, trim, softly angular, knifed into the water. The immense shining undersides of a plane passing overhead reflected on the pleated, cold-looking water. The river was moving fast, the current boiling up the muddy bottom in cinnamon-coloured clouds. Pale rising sunshine made the riverbank broken gold.

Dreaming of painkillers in the floating bow, I remembered drawing Nan as she watched the snooker.

I didn't know I was an outsider until Evelyn Crow called me one.

Among the gleaming vitrines.

I just lived in the world I lived in with everybody else.

All of us struggling to get by, as Nan would have said.

I gave her *Great Expectations* and she said, I can't read that.

Some other idea of myself there.

Punk was a help. Set me right.

Friday nights Nan sat with the men in the public bar.

After she died I went out into the country, drawing. It barely needs justifying. It's as old as singing.

House and all the other houses gone. Knocked down. Everything gone. Way of life.

I drew travellers, squatters, runaways, unemployed blokes.

Geezers in pubs. Pawnbrokers, pound shops, the bookies, churches.

Drew the pub the pub the pub the pub.

Empty factories, demos, riot cops busting heads.

Plastic blue mattress, locked door.

Winos in doorways. Sleeping standing up.

Cars with different coloured doors, rubbish, dogs.

Paintings of post-industrial desolation, Crow had called them. Damaged and fractured.

From the gone world.

The dogs don't know what they are, Adam said. Long ago they might have been something, but now you couldn't put a name to them.

Bloody mongrels, he said. That's what they are.

There were four in the box, two black and white, one all over tan and one tan and white. The tan and white dog had one white sock and three white rings around three ankles. She had a tail with a white tip like a fox brush.

A black and white dog ran back and forth by the river-bank, snapping at parcels of froth the onshore wind was making airborne, the froth alien and white in the lead-grey late afternoon. The dog stalked the white foam, her pointed ears raised, ruffled body hunched with tension that was released when she lunged, jaws snapping.

Adam put the box down. The pups moved over each other, blinking, making soft effortful noises from the back of their throats. A warm biscuit smell came from the box.

You want a dog? he said.

They were so small. I put my hand in the box and the pups mouthed and nipped at it with their sharp, unbeliev-ably white teeth. I pushed their fur back against the grain and gently pulled their tiny ears. I put my hand on the belly of the fattest one, the tan and white dog, and it was hot with the blood of new life.

No mate, I said.

The old man been looking after you?

Look after myself.

Fool me.

Never asked for your help, I said.

Grinding pain. Beginning low in my spine and tunnelling up my back and down my legs. Pain that varied its route and intensity from moment to moment. Anger rode along if allowed. I was made of sullen, badly fused blocks of self that I heard crunching against one another whenever I moved.

Didn't go mad then, cut your ear off.

Fuck off.

The tan and white dog bit my finger.

What'll you do if you can't get rid of them, I said.

I'm not trying to get rid of them, he said, I'm trying to find them homes.

What if you can't.

Drown them in the river, the big youth said, his eyes shining, what do you think?

That mum? I said, nodding at the dog on the riverbank.

That's mum, Adam said.

What's she think about you giving her pups away?

Maybe she thinks it's easier than looking after them all, Adam said.

The old tyres used for fenders squeaked against each other and made the pups open their eyes wide. They climbed and rolled and mouthed each other in the box that was lined with a clean-looking red flannel shirt.

The old man came into my wheelhouse without knocking. Raised his hand and took off his wool hat. I hadn't heard him coming, or felt his presence changing the movement of the always moving boats.

Wrong to say that sound travelled a long way on the island. Clear days it did. Still days. When you could hear a stone whisper. But since I'd arrived I could count on one hand the number of clear and still days. Sometimes it rained so hard I wouldn't have heard bloody murder happening on the next boat.

Adam was right. For days after falling it was all I could do to wipe my own arse without screaming. I couldn't sleep. Shouted and raged. No more, I said over and over.

Locked in a cell all you can do about the screams you hear is to ignore them. Can't help anybody. Youth prison is the worst, borstal. I was in a place called Send. Doesn't take much and I'm back there. Every night you'd hear somebody breaking or being broken. Drugs kicking in too much, or not enough. More than once the screams came from inside my own head. With no love for God you pray for it to stop. Promise anything. See anybody dead if they don't fucking stop.

Shut the fuck up, somebody shouts, fore I give you something to fucking cry about.

Sometimes it stops. There's a loud silence. You finally fall asleep. A chair being kicked over wakes you, the sound of choking. Alarms shatter against the cold walls.

—

I camped out in the wheelhouse.

Murder getting up there, but better than going mad stuck below all day. The dark closed-in feeling.

The old man still crossed my boat twice a day. I watched him. Wrapped in sour blankets and the clothes I never changed, because it was too painful to try. Pens and paper in my lap. Ready.

I began to see him. The skin tight against the shape of his skull, so that the evenly proportioned features, lead-coloured eyes, high cheekbones, wide nose, were not what I remembered when he was gone. Instead I thought of a surface rocky and unyielding. The colour of damp sandstone. A face formed for privacy, so used to hiding its secrets and hurts that the contrary was true. The old man radiated strong feeling.

The Perspex window, most often blurred with rain, was a barrier between all the things I thought and wondered about him, and my inability to raise my hand.

He saw me and thought about me, too. Had to. Looked straight at me with a stone face.

From the start after my fall I was worried about the portaloo. Lifting it. Taking it all that way to the cesspit. To put off needing to lug the full container up the steps and into the forest, I sometimes went over the side of the boat at night, muffling the sound as best I could by pissing on the fenders, against the side of the boat, anywhere but directly into the water. Shivering in the cold. Trying not to wet the blanket.

Couldn't put it off forever. Didn't want to ask for help. Adam, Stella. Do it myself, fuck it.

Managed to drag the heavy shit container out of the tiny shower unit, sloshing and bumping it across the floor.

Tried to lift it and climb the steps at the same time. Stupid. Fell down hard and yelled like a bastard.

The old man's face had appeared at the top of the wheelhouse steps and looked down at me.

I was brought up to believe that God tempered the wind to the shorn lamb, he'd said.

The old man nodded at Adam without really looking at him. He was fixed on the box of pups. Rubbing his thick hands together. The tan and white dog looked back at him and sounded like she was humming.

Let me see those dogs, John Rose said.

John Rose's dog lay asleep on my wheelhouse floor, the tan of her coat fiery in the light. The big window gathered and contained to the space we sat in the April sun. River a smooth brightness. Metallic seabirds flashed upstream.

The young dog's lips were drawn back from her teeth, exposing her pink and liver gums, and she was growling and yipping in her sleep. Twelve weeks old or thereabouts, her green feet paddling and softly brushing against the wood floor.

Why don't you take the blessed dog out? John had said, the two of them at my door before I'd had coffee.

John looked me up and down.

Stuck in here all winter, he said.

Turning back like he'd left the stove on.

Dog near enough bouncing up and down, barking happily.

In the forest, the winged fruit of ash trees parachuting down all around, the dog had jumped into a water hole thick with algae. In the warm wheelhouse she smelled strongly sulphurous. Green stains hid her one white sock and the white rings around her ankles. The tip of her tail was green.

John wrinkled his nose and looked down at the dog. The heat of the light she was lying in made the bad egg smell stronger.

Why you let her jump in the stink?

She never asked me, I said.

Contrails blossomed then disappeared across the window-framed sky.

A partly inflated plastic bag on the water glowed with captured sunshine as it moved downstream. Insects fizzed just above the surface, promoting fish to rise, the patterns of their rising spreading and vanishing on the water. Below the surface were dark locomotive shadows in turns visible and not as the fish returned to deeper water.

A small colony of goldfinches had settled or returned to the trees near my boat, and I could hear their high liquid singing even through the closed wheelhouse door. I had thought of feeding them but they were doing fine without my help. They were getting fatter by the day.

Never spent time alone with a dog before. Steered clear. Living rough you met a million dogs. Some friendly, some not. I was worried she'd run off. Home in one piece. What more did John want? Laughed when she snapped her jaws at falling ash fruit bouncing off her nose.

Coming out of the forest, people I didn't know and hadn't spoken to smiled at the dog and me with her. I felt the muscles in my face soften, my clamped mouth relax. I looked down and smiled at the dog.

People sat on their boats, on battered camp chairs turned to the sun, though it was not yet warm enough to go without a fire inside.

Winter clothes and bedding brought up to air, narrow-boats crowned with folded mattresses. Thin columns of woodsmoke.

The boy Danny waved and yelled: Terry!

Jumping over the gangplank and coming to hug the dog.

She's wet and smelly, I said.

The boy stuck his face in her fur.

Mmmmmmn, Danny said.

The dog sitting patiently, letting the boy love her.

You like the coffee? John said.

It was phenomenal.

It's all right, I said.

John had brought me back from the dead with his magic brew. When he found me down there with the shitter.

John had lifted the heavy container and stood it upright. Tightened the cap.

Sit up son, he'd said.

I'm a grown man, I said.

I came to know his embrace. Sweet breath. The reefer coat like worn steel wool. Hands were old tools. The island seal of woodsmoke, damp, the special impress of boat life. Some other faint astringent. Not turpentine. Sharper, a bit on the nose.

Now the old man looked at me across his coffee. Light flared in his eyes. He looked at the dog.

You are not the only one with no sense, he said. And who needs a bath.

The dog yipped in her sleep but didn't move. Like the goldfinches, I could almost see her growing.

No drink since Christmas. Knew enough to be careful. Been here before.

I'd made a ton of drawings. The dog dappled by sunlight, bursting through the ground cover of ferns. Diving cormorants, goldfinches. The always-changing, unrepeatable light on the water. Always the same, always different. In a drawer I had a book full of many versions of John. Never shown him.

Don't think you're coming home like that, John said.

The dog looked up from her place on the floor, just lifting her head to gaze blankly at him and then lying back down. From the neck down she didn't move. Within seconds she was dreaming again.

Phew, John said to her. What a damn stink.

Slowly I got down on the floor. Tried not to make any noise. Moans and groans. Wasn't done. Stretched myself out next to the dog. Just trying to move the pain around. Put one hand on the dog's warm fur. She sighed in her sleep. You'd have to think, his age, that John was in pain all the time.

It's about Vesna? I said.

John's wife.

There was an open envelope next to John on the banquette. The old man handed it to me.

John had told me about Vesna but I didn't have it all clear.

Why was he paying somebody to look for two women whose names he didn't know?

Because they are the bitches who kill her! he'd shouted.

Gave her morphine. Hid her phone. Stole her money. Care home workers. Zero hours contracts. Disappeared. Not known under the names given. All bones, breath and eyes, Vesna. So thin the joints showed through. Teeth standing out like a starved horse. Leukaemia. Died anyway. Not the point.

From the owner, John said, looking at the envelope like it was responsible for the sulphurous stink.

The care home?

The old man sat back on the banquette, holding his elbow, the palm of his other hand facing upwards, a storyteller of working harbours. The river moved beneath the boat. A kind of leaning. I was beginning to understand how the tide worked. When it turned. It was turning now. John reached down and touched my boot.

No, he said, of this place.

John's irises seemed to lack definition, rims indistinct, crumbling almost.

Read it, he said.

Company headed paper. Kaplan International. Two paragraphs. As of September the mooring fees were going up by £250 a quarter. Certain improvements. Cover the costs.

Typed. I turned the letter over. The back was blank.

What's Kaplan International? I said.

In the late afternoon the sky and water were burnt orange.

The sun was falling into the river. A black cloud of

starlings appeared downstream, backlit by fire. Their shapeshifting protection against predators.

Alex Kaplan owns the island, John said.

The Kaplan who was shot?

That man, John said. Yes, used to promote fighters. You know him?

I've heard of him, I said.

Vesna and me knew his father, John said. Mr Kaplan had a big house across the river. Spent most of his time here. Paid for the upkeep. Charged almost nothing for mooring. But he died. Alex Kaplan got the big house and has not spent a penny on this place. Waiting. Every summer more people visit here. They like to think they discover the place.

Now this Kaplan thinks it is the time to spend some money. Clean the place up. Make it nice for the visitors, proper showers and toilets, a place that sells food, but make us pay for it, or make us leave.

Leave?

Of course leave! John said. My God! You think people here have two hundred and fifty pound sitting around doing nothing? A thousand a year?

People will leave. They'll have to either way. Some might leave rather than give Kaplan any more damn money.

Why now? I said.

The world had turned velvet, and darkness filled the wheelhouse. With the sun gone, the wheelhouse was no longer warm. I should have saved them for emergencies, but I got up and lit a couple of candles rather than turn on the light.

John glanced at me, then tested his lower lip with his teeth. Looked down at his thick hands. Raised them fractionally and then let them rest in his lap.

Spite, he said at last. Revenge.

Revenge for what? I said.

John didn't answer.

The candles guttered. The boat was old. Perhaps some as yet unknown separation of the planking. Maybe a tear, thin as a knife edge, in the hold.

The button on the control panel, ruby in the candlelight, reminded me I had not pumped the bilges in a while.

Alex Kaplan had made a full recovery after a fighter he managed named Millar shot him with an old-fashioned revolver. Kaplan hadn't pressed charges, got out of the fight game. Much was made of Brady Millar's unusual background for a fighter. Been to university and was an army officer before turning professional. Millar later disappeared. Nobody on either side talked, but everybody supposed Kaplan had wronged Brady Millar somehow. I was painting fighters then, and heard Kaplan sometimes bought pictures, that's why I was interested. The word around the gyms was that this Kaplan was a dangerous man.

John went to the open door and looked out. The dog watched him from the floor.

I worked in this country all my life, the old man said. Blown out of the water on this country's damn business. Alex Kaplan tells me I have to choose. Justice for my wife, or keep my home.

She'd want you to be happy, I said.

You never met her, John shouted, how the damn hell you going to know what she want?

Picking up his hat and going out the door. He did not call the dog and she didn't follow him, but lay back down, staring at the empty space where he'd been.

John kept an ancient tender tied to his barge, a little flat-bottomed Zodiac, and I heard him take the boat out onto the river, late as it was. I went outside and stood on the stern deck, looking downstream. The moon was rising, and John followed the path it made on the water until he disappeared from my sight. The sound of the outboard diminished until I knew he was far out in the river's deep midwater channel. Then John must have switched off the engine, as I could hear the heavy beating wings of a pair of swans coming in low over the river from the west, looking for a place to land. The swans were luminescent in the moonlight, their high moving whiteness fading as they passed into the night. It was a long time before John's outboard started up again and I saw the old tender coming back. The dog came to stand at my side. Made no sound.

Good girl, I said.

The dog leaped from my boat to the empty barge, and then ran and jumped again, landing noiselessly outside John's cabin door, her tail a bright pennant in the darkness. I followed her.

John?

Under the quarter moon and starry sky, the tenement of boats rocked on the changing tide. Mooring ropes tightened then slackened off. The groaning of fenders and timber under strain sounded above the constant gloopy chorus of water against boat, boat against water.

The moon-soaked painted colours of John's boat were rich and deep. The English rose was almost black. The castle was dark and shining.

Lush sounds from inside. Music. A woman's voice.

John, I called again.

Dog pushed her way in.

The old man put whisky in his coffee sometimes. Grease the wheels, he said. When he'd had a couple under his belt his eyes would light up and he'd tell me sea stories. Never anything about however many years he'd spent on an assembly line.

John? You there?

I'd imagined a stateroom of fitted wood, brass navigation instruments shining in muted light. Sextants, chronometer. Charts. A pink map held flat by heavy coins, bearing the likenesses of forgotten rulers of renamed lands. Trophies. An opium pipe. A shrunken tattooed head.

I'm coming in.

Wine vinegar. The boat reeked of it. Damp that had turned to mould, and the vinegar John was using to fight back. The bulkheads where they met the overhead, the galley, every surface I could see, was marked by black mould and the signs of John's cleaning. Everything in the boat was squared away. But it was all threatened by the creeping fungi.

Rich sea captains gilded mould to show their wealth.

In a black iron stove the blaze of a new fire was yet to settle. John still had his coat on. Didn't see us. Holding Kaplan's letter in his hand. Instructions from upriver. John standing like a man given an order he can't carry out. Big-knuckled, thick-fingered hands that were never still, but always testing the physical world around him.

The music was too loud for the small space.

A woman's voice. Promising or asking for a little loving in the morning.

John?

The old man yelled: Michael!

You made me damn jump.

Brought your dog back.

The blessed dog's right here.

Pile of old blankets by the fire but the dog had already jumped up on the settee and was grinning at John. The old man sat down next to her. Almost let himself fall.

Looked around at his things like he didn't know who they belonged to.

Shelves fitted to the bulkhead on the river side. LPs in plastic covers, the seams edged in mould.

Photographs, also beaded by mould. Books that looked like they'd been rescued from a flood, then dried over a smoking fire. Young John standing next to a lifeboat davit on the deck of a ship. Snow covering the canvas over the lifeboat and crowning the davit. John giving nothing away under a pencil moustache, wrapped in a reefer coat and wearing a watch cap, hugging himself, snow falling all around, the snowballs that had hit him visible as small, violent marks of whiteness on his coat and face.

Not a captain. Course not.

A middle-aged woman in blue overalls. Dirty blonde hair tied up with a red scarf. John next to her. The woman was smiling at a long-haired, dark-eyed boy who was about thirteen or fourteen. Streak of paint across his smooth cheek. The three of them holding up paintbrushes. Big grins from everybody.

A girl wearing lots of eyeliner and a graduation cap and gown. Standing next to the blonde woman. John not there. The girl not smiling. The picture not straight. Damp had got inside the frame, and some of the girl's face – a cheek, her unhappy, angry eyes – were stuck to the glass that had also been stained by damp.

John shoved the dog off the settee.

She jumped straight back up and snuggled into him.

You spoil the blasted dog, John said, finding a biscuit in his pocket and giving it to her.

Saw me looking at the photograph of the unhappy girl.

Got up slowly. Straightened the picture with a thick hand.

Your daughter? I said.

John made a noise that could have been a yes or a no. Turned to the record player as if he'd just realized it was playing. Made a sour face.

Lifted the needle from the record and it stopped.

Vesna's favourite, he said.

Dusty in Memphis.

Went around turning lamps off, so that we sat within the light made by the fire.

I never cared for it that much, the old man said.

Who's Michael? I said.

John spoke softly in the ticking silence.

Boy was either drawing you, the old man said, or jumping out of a tree trying to scare you to death.

John held up his hand palm out. Don't interrupt.

Vesna liked to say, there's only room on the boat for the things we love, he said. Spent years working on her, weekends, why not enjoy it. Nancy – John turned to where the girl looked out accusingly through the glass – had left home to study. I'd stopped work. Been stopped. Made sense. Pack up the house and come here. A fresh start.

The dog stretched out all four feet in her sleep. She was lying upside down next to John, her head flung back like her neck was broken, eyes closed, an edge of pink tongue showing between her teeth. She stretched to the limit, all four feet raised, toes spread, her ribcage sharply convex, her stomach a valley. John put his hand around her muzzle and gently shook it, then moved his hand and smoothed back her ears. The dog yawned enormously, her young white teeth like pins. She smacked her jaws and rolled over onto her side. Gave John's hand a lick, fell back asleep.

The first years were tough, John said.

Michael helped. The boy make you smile. A headful of curls. Cheeky. A roaming spirit. Perseis was just a silly damned hippy. Vesna helped the girl because that is what Vesna is like. Gene I believe love the boy but Gene is fierce. I tried to tell him. And before you know it the boy was growing. Becoming a teenager. It was Vesna he went to for guidance.

John looked up at the mould on the deckhead.

The boat got sick the same time as my wife, he said. This damn mould creep up while she was in the hospital. Michael tried to help, but he was distracted, and upset about Vesna.

John blinked.

Vesna die. Killed. Like I told you. Never mind the damn cancer. Three years ago. My daughter came here, once, and told me all the bad things I am, then went away and never come back. And for a while I don't care about anything. Not me, not the boat, not Michael. I even hit that boy once. For acting up. Just a clip. Not learned a blasted thing. I hear Vesna saying that to me. All the time. The boy was just missing me, I hear her say. The same as you, she says. But it wasn't the same.

John closed his eyes. Sat like that until I thought he'd fallen asleep. Finally he looked at me again.

The boy drowned, John said, two years ago next summer. Just a youth. A terrible thing.

I started to say something.

Listen to what I'm telling you, John said. Policemen come with dogs. Divers. Drag ropes. They question everybody. Go harder on some than others. Gene. The police are hard on Gene.

There was a red-headed girl, John said. Michael and her were together. Alexandra Kaplan.

Kaplan?

Alex Kaplan's daughter. The police question her once. They talk to Kaplan, and then he tell them what he was going to do. And he did. Took the girl away, out of the country.

The police keep after Gene, John said. Grew up in a boys' home. Was in trouble as a youth. Stealing cars, fighting and this and that. Gene won't go quietly. Talk to Alex Kaplan, he tells them, ask him about his girl. The police don't give up on Gene. They come for him again the other day. I saw the launch. They take him and sweat him for a couple of days, then they bring him back.

The old man pulled the sleeve of his coat over his hand and opened the little door of the stove. Poked at the burning wood. Made the sparks fly.

What do they think Gene knows? I said.

Michael's body has never been found, John said. The boy

never come out of the river. Maybe somebody gave the police ideas.

Wood cracked in the iron stove.

Gene's gone wild, John said. We have to forgive him. To lose a child. Like that. No body to lay to rest.

John put his rough hand on the dog's flank. Pushed his hand hard through her fur until the dog raised her head and stared at him. John lifted his hand. The dog lay down. Sighed.

You think this is why Kaplan is moving now?

I think Alex Kaplan is a man who likes to get all his birds in a row, the old man said. Before he take out his gun.

The forest was deeper than it seemed from the outside. The dog ran away from me. Flash of red. Into the trees. Across the invisible line between any forest I might come to know, and the place where she was born.

Tried to catch up. Had to stop. Hands on knees coughing and spitting on the ground. I couldn't travel fast or without pain and I didn't know where I was going. The path had taken me away from my home clearings and dells. The ground seemed to be rising.

Unfamiliar bluebells shone in the dark. From somewhere came the sounds of sawing and hammering.

Shouted for the dog, but either she couldn't hear me over the noise of the camp dogs barking, or the summons in that barking was stronger than mine. One of the dogs was likely to be her mother.

She might run into the big saw I could hear, or be attacked by any of the wild animals I imagined would be living in the forest. Weasels. Badgers. Bloody snakes probably.

Spat again. Forced myself to breathe deeply. Stood up straight. Called the dog again, shouting loud this time. Birds rose from the trees surrounding me, crows and the bright parakeets that John told me had been colonizing the island for years, growing in number and forcing out the indigenous birds.

Followed the barking. Light through the trees promised clearer ground. A couple of bin bags were tied and looped over a branch at head height. A rain barrel. A shallow pit half filled with empty tins and bottles. Barking close by and a man's voice. The dog came back to collect me, looking up happily before turning back where she'd come from.

Good girl, I said. Good girl.

Into a clearing busy with welcoming dogs.

Can't control your dog.

The homeless giant was shirtless, his upper body hugely pale except for his chest. He was sitting on a camp chair in front of a smoking fire pit. Three other mismatched chairs around the fire. Tarpaulin shelter behind him. Adam's black trousers and boots were still thick with winter mud. A quilted plaid shirt hung on the back of his chair. Black and blue.

Adam reached around for the shirt on the back of his chair and put it on. Not before I saw a huge, raised, violet welt, like a pressed burn, running across Adam's chest from shoulder to shoulder.

The shelter was held up internally by a network of criss-crossed branches lashed together, from which were hanging a dozen or more plastic bags containing, I guessed, Adam's clothes and other possessions.

A camp bed that looked too small. A tough plastic box next to some boots, with a handle and a meshed door, and a big sticker on the side that read *Live Animals* in green letters. Plastic washbowl with various bottles of supermarket shower gel and shampoo. An old fruit box filled with tins of food.

Everything, inside and outside the shelter, was covered in dried mud though you could see attempts had been made to remove the worst of it.

In the trees I could see a mud-streaked green tent, just big enough for two people.

Two worn sleeping bags had been put out to air over low branches. There was a hole in one of them and stuffing was sticking out.

A small yellow generator with a battered laptop plugged in. The big fire pit was fringed with thick drifts of ghostly grey ash. Inside the ring were blackened pieces of glowing and smoking wood. At the centre of the pit a small flame edged in blue. Smoke rose perfectly straight before dispersing in the air over our heads. Ariel Galton had once written: the vertical line is disclosed by a hollyhock, or a column of woodsmoke.

John's dog went straight to the giant-sized youth and he held her and rubbed her head and cooed to her. The other dogs began crowding in.

Not my dog, I said. As you know.

Why you with her if she's not your dog?

Needed to see you.

You got lost, your dog got away.

Still, I said, here I am.

I heard you calling her.

Adam's hair was loose and to his shoulders. He had a

loose end of it in his mouth as though as he was sucking the moisture from it. Big drops of water shone brightly in his beard.

John's had a notice, I said.

Chewing his hair he jabbed his scarred and battered face at me.

I heard about it. What's that got to do with me?

If you've heard about it then you know.

What?

It's bad news.

He reached into a top pocket of his shirt and fetched out an elastic band. Squeezed out the water from his hair, scraped and tied it back. Wiped his hands on his trousers.

Nothing's gonna happen, he said.

Can't be living here for nothing, I said. You'll be the first they come for.

Get up in the fucking trees then.

Seen this before, I said. Know how it ends.

A man with a skull for a face walked out from the tree-line, holding a plastic bottle of clear liquid. Gene. Eyes as huge and as dark as I remembered. Boots heavy with mud. Dirty green combat trousers with a thick leather belt. Doing up his zipper as he stepped out. Big carabiner shackle through the belt loop just above the left pocket of his trousers, with a chain attached to it that disappeared into the pocket. Black hoodie, no dirtier than mine, with the sleeves rolled up. Chevrons of savage and barely healed cuts made angry pink bars on the inside of his left arm.

Big home-made India ink tattoo on his right arm.

Thick outline of a broken heart with the initials 'M. V.' inside it.

Cunts will make you pay for the air you breathe, he said.

Face a death's head. What you needed to know about him was in those black eyes. There was something moving in them, too fast and too far back to identify what it was.

You got a letter? I said.

Gene's eyes widened even further and he stuck out his chin.

Fuck's a letter? he said. Fucking nada. The coppers.

Looked at the bottle in his hands. Took a swig. Held out the bottle.

Take a drink, Gene said.

Petrol on a fire. The burning stink flooding the inside of my head. Shorten your life, whatever it was.

I held up my hand.

No thanks, I said.

Take a bloody drink, Gene said.

I won't, I said. Thanks.

Won't? Gene said.

The look he gave me scraped against my backbone.

No.

Too good for a bit of Tuppy's? Gene said, pushing my shoulder with an iron hand.

What's the matter? he said. This stuff's fucking organic mate, fucking craft, fucking artisan. That's what cunts like you drink, no?

Pushed me again. Same place. Harder.

The dogs lying in the weak sun raised their heads and stared at us.

Keep still. Head down. Show my hands. Unarmed. What you're supposed to do. Hope danger passes. Not in prison, street. Wouldn't last five minutes. Not here.

Shoved Gene and grabbed his neck in one motion. Hard grip. Felt his throat, the thick arteries in his neck, pulsing and warm under my hand. Walked him backwards.

Fucking problem? I said.

Black eyes. Nothing. Wasn't scared. Didn't give a shit. When I looked down John's dog was by my side, looking at Gene with her ears back. She barked. Rest of the dogs were fanned out close behind her.

Give it up Gene, Adam said, laughing. Turned the fucking dogs against you.

Let him go, Terry.

I stayed where I was. Fuck you as well.

Make it count. Step in. Fuck him if he spent the night in the cells. Make him wish he fucking stayed there. Forced myself to breathe in and out. Deep breaths. Until the heavy roar began to slow down. Lost a kid. Fuck's sake. Let go of him. Not his fault you hurt all over.

John Rose's dog licked my hand.

Gene started to move his hands to rub his neck and stopped. Poured a splash of the poteen or whatever it was on the ground before he took another drink.

Gene, Adam said, his big hand trailing in the fur of the dogs that flowed past and round him like water.

Gene held his hands out and the dogs came to him,

snuffling his palms. He rubbed their heads, never taking his eyes off me.

Come and sit down Gene, Adam said. Terry.

I saw Gene go somewhere, and I did not know where that place was. Never been there and didn't want to. Then he came back, slowly at first and then all at once. Gene sat down. I did too, leaving the third camp chair empty between us.

Anybody got a smoke? he said.

I handed over my makings. We smoked in silence. Gene threw his end in the fire. Sat rolling the clear bottle between his hands.

Tuppy? I said.

Tuppy Lawrence, Gene said. Got a still on his boat. Tastes like piss haha.

Gene took another drink, a big one. Tears in his eyes afterwards. Sat down. Warming himself at the fire. Huge clouds moved slowly in the clearing of sky above our heads, coming together, joining, breaking apart. Crows travelled between the high treetops, calling in faraway voices. The dogs that had been lying in the sun sat up while it was gone, waiting for the poor warmth to return.

Cop said to me, where were you when it happened? Gene said. How many times I got to tell you, I said. I wasn't there. Don't know when it happened. Know somebody who did, who was fucking there, why don't you talk to them? Cop said, when did you last see Michael?

All the time, Gene said, voice low. My son. Michael's standing here right now.

From nowhere a knife with a jagged edge appeared in

Gene's hand. Something you'd use to cut fishing line. Gene leaned forward and jammed the knife point first in the dirt in front of him.

Fucking told him, he said. You won't ask Kaplan questions I'll talk to him my fucking self.

Gene stabbed at the ground. Digging out a small hollow, the dirt flaring from his knife. The knife scraping on stone.

Cop said, are you making threats, Mr Vincent?

Digging into the dirt with his knife.

Cops won't put the divers in again. Find him. Won't put 'em in. Said he's not in the river. Said where is he then? Said his body's on the island, Mr Vincent. Reason to believe. I said you what? Turned over every stone, I said, looking for him. Bare hands. Think I haven't? My boy?

Gene hit his chest hard with the fist that held the knife.

Said you're a violent ex-offender, Mr Vincent. Said that's why I fucking come here in the first place. Get away from who I was.

Don't fucking listen, Gene said, looking down at his closed fist, the knife. Think I did it. Cop said.

Shaking his head.

Said if it was the rich girl in the river you'd never stop looking for her.

I couldn't see his face. Voice rising slowly from a far place, deep inside, somewhere under blackness. Knife hand stabbing deeper in the dirt.

Gene, Adam said. Mate.

I'd met Perseis walking in the forest under the last full moon.

Couldn't sleep. Wanted a drink. Went for a walk instead. Winter rain still filled the muddy hollows between the trees, and the churned-up ground, the reflective surface water, was a darkly shining honeycomb, its solidity uncertain every time I put my foot down. The trees were blue columns. The river was silver movement between the trees.

Found myself at Michael's stones. Sat down. Wondered if I should smoke. The dog was not with me, otherwise I'd have known Perseis was coming long before she entered the clearing, wearing a midnight-blue cloak, and carrying a flat stone in her hands. The long hem of the cloak was soaking, her face and violet eyes moon-washed under the soft hood.

I took the stone from her. Seemed the thing to do. Cold, smooth. Darkness retreating from its surface as it dried. Put it down on top of the others. Perseis looked down at the configuration of stones, moved the new stone a fraction, nodded. She took down her hood. With her cropped head and violet eyes she looked like a believer in a cause I recognized but could not name.

The painter, she said.

Terry.

You've come from Paris? she said.

Paris? I said.

Did he send for me?

Who?

Michael of course, she said.

She held out her empty arms, standing still, palms upward, as though testing for rain that did not fall, but had been and gone though more was promised. Later I thought

80

of her that way, held in the time both before and after the rain fell. The air dry, the water on the ground a mystery to her.

Nan by the end spoke in different voices. Napoo finny. She'd look at me and say that like I was supposed to understand. Ariel Galton turned her visions into paintings that peeled my skin. I talked to these dead women as much as if not more than I talked to anybody else. Maybe in her dreams John's dog took other forms.

The dog was wrestling now with one of her black and white brothers. Taking it in turns to force each other to the ground. John's dog kicked out as she lay on her back, the black and white dog play-biting her throat. Both dogs grunting with effort. Then John's dog was up suddenly, as though on a signal, and driving her brother down. The floor of the camp had been roughly swept within the last day or so and was mostly packed dirt. John's dog shook herself, and particles of the ground were visible as a fine mist in the sunshine that still reached us in the clearing.

Been home since they let you go? Adam said.

Came straight here, Gene said.

They looked at each other. Finally Adam nodded.

I love her, the skull-faced man said. That's the fucking problem. Sun comes up with her every morning.

Gene pulled his knife from the dirt, wiped the blade on his trouser leg and folded it and put the knife in his pocket. Swept the dirt back in the hole.

Not enough, he said, laughing with no joy. Long fucking chalk.

Gene stood and walked towards me. I began to get up but he went on past, banging my shoulder hard with his knee as he did so. Walked into the treeline and disappeared.

Adam looked into the fire.

Police turned his boat upside down when it happened, he said. Divers crawling around in the muck underneath. Brought dogs on board. Searched all over the island. Put Gene in a room for days. Sweated him. Meanwhile the girl, the only witness, flies to Switzerland.

She's back now.

Yes she is, Adam said, and Old Bill are putting the screws to Gene again.

I took out my tin and rolled another cigarette. Handed the tin to Adam. Adam held a stick to the fire until it was flaming and then lit us both. I watched the dogs playing in the fading dappled light.

Perseis asked me if I'd seen Michael, I said. In Paris. I've never been to Paris in my life.

All her people are in Paris, Adam said. Cut her off when she took up with Gene, least that's what he told me. I don't know if she's ever told them about Michael.

That he died? I said.

I don't know if she told them about him at all.

Gene got no people?

Adam shook his head.

She knows he's gone, he said. Gene reckons she says all that Paris stuff so she won't say what she really thinks.

Which is what?

That Gene had something to do with it.

Gene really believe that?

Explain why Gene looked like he was being eaten away from the inside.

She needs to believe her son will come back alive, Adam said. That's a big part of it I reckon.

Plenty of people had made money from that lie. Nan cleaned the spiritualist church, a big brick church in its own grounds, with a black-painted iron fence all the way round.

People come to talk to their dead, Nan said, but the dead don't talk for free.

I never stop wanting her to come back, and she does come back, in the shape of a head that was like hers, a southern voice. She came back, in my cell, my locked ward and on the road. She never goes away and she never comes back.

I'm not who you think I am, I'd said to Perseis.

Then why are you here? she said.

For the light, I'd said.

No, Perseis said, gesturing with her hands at the clearing, the small tower of stones.

Why are you here?

The sun was below the tops of the trees now, moving slowly west. Sunlight still found us, in flashing parcels, but it was darker and cooler in the camp. We rolled and smoked more cigarettes. Adam always knew where all the dogs were.

You working? I said.

Always working. Worked on half those bloody towers.

Doing what?

Got two jobs, the big youth said with a half smile. This and that.

Gene?

Boats. Build 'em, fix 'em. Keep 'em running. Good bloke. It's a bloody shame.

Adam reached behind himself for more wood for the fire. He held a piece to the flames, blowing and stirring it until the fire glowed, and then he lay the wood on the fire with another piece crossways. Sat looking into the flames. Then up at me.

You never asked for them painkillers, Adam said.

It was a long winter, I said.

Adam had become a dark figure rimmed in low light. He kept adding wood until the fire was blazing. The dogs had gathered to the heat and were lying down, staring at the flames.

Could still smell the strong drink. The poteen or whatever it was. Tuppy, Gene had said. I wondered where his boat was. Not at the moorings.

When I woke up it was dark. The blaze had quietened, and the fire pit was a low bowl of pulsing heat. Adam was asleep, sparks making little smoking holes in his trousers. The broken parts of his face and head seemed softened, and I could see how young he was. The half-wild dogs were asleep. Five sets of eyes snapping open the second I moved. Adam opened his eyes and looked at me.

Take your bloody dog with you, he said.

Not my dog.

I turned to look for her. She was right there, looking up at my face. Eyes shining, mouth open. Ready.

I don't know what you're looking for, Terry, Adam said. But you're not the story here.

Your trousers are on fire, I said.

It was full dark in the forest, though there was a slim curve of silver that flashed irregularly at the edge of my vision, on the right side, and that may have been the result of the fall in winter, or even some unknown light source hidden and revealed by the trees and the spaces between them. I worried that I had got turned around, and that the light was coming from Adam's fire, but the dog did not hesitate or doubt her direction, and I followed her, the tip of her tail bright in the darkness.

It's as you would expect, John Rose said when I took the dog back.

A few can pay, he said. They'll moan but some might be glad to get rid of the riff-raff. Most can't afford it though, and don't know what to do. The renters know something's up, rumours, but nobody's had a letter. A lot of them live on boats that aren't worth what they're paying now. The owners will most likely cut their losses, kick off the people living there and sell the boats for scrap.

It was the moon, of course. In the forest.

Terry, he said. Boy, are you listening?

It make you feel worthless, he said. Like your life never mattered.

The canvas was warm to touch and hot under my bare feet.

From the top of John's boat, I could see a pair of swans on the other side of the river, spaced parallel on the water. Holding their positions on the gently running tide. In the space between them I could see the smudged marks of four downy cygnets.

The black canvas covering was tied down by bungee cords, and came off in sections.

Fold each piece in four, John called from the other end of the boat.

The cords were stretched tight and hard and soaked through. Nipped my fingers more than once trying to release the hooks, rusty where the protective covering of plastic had worn away.

I moved and worked slowly, carefully, my body still sore from my winter fall.

Above the swans the willows that fringed the riverbank. Through the willows the private jetties, and above the jetties emerald lawns sloping up to the big houses. White stone villas with red tile roofs. Reflected sunlight blazed from a conservatory window.

I stood on the barge barefoot and shirtless, my trousers rolled up.

I could see a long-legged girl in T-shirt and shorts, sitting on a patterned blanket in a garden, the redness of her hair and white skin clearly visible. Somebody must have called her, as all at once she jumped up, then bent to gather her blanket. She skipped and then stopped herself, before walking slowly out of my sight, the blanket under her arm, her hair aflame.

Vesna used to make a big thing about taking the covers off, John said.

I bet, I said.

John glared at me and then laughed.

A week at least of uninterrupted sun before the old man had said: Are you up to giving me a hand?

Put it that way I can't say no.

The top of the barge was not much wider than my shoulders. Difficult to stay balanced while removing the thick canvas from under my feet.

From up there I could see the beginnings of deep green inner space below the river's surface. Valleys among the reeds and river grass leading down to blackness. Perch rose for waterboatmen.

John was also barefoot. Wearing blue overalls with several buttons undone, and a white vest bright against his skin. No hat. Straight and strong as a length of rebar, was how he looked. Sun out. Different man. Must have been something when he was younger. Dressed for shore leave in wild port cities that were only names in books to me. Aden and San Francisco. Mombasa, Port Moresby.

At mid-river spangles of light were arranged in long bars, squares or unnamed shapes flashing in endless random sequence. I wondered if Michael had been carried away into that light. If that's how it happened. I was standing where in previous summers the boy would surely once have stood, helping John.

Parakeets zoomed from the treeline making the alarm cry they made. The dog barked from inside John's boat. Between these sounds I could hear wood pigeons, softly reverberative, the clicks and caws of the crows. Above the trees, woodsmoke from the camp slowly dispersed. A cooking fire. The smoke rose, was visible and then not, returning as a harsh perfume at the back of my throat. An engine fired into life out of sight.

A motorboat roared into view through the curtain of willows. Behind a high transparent windscreen, the man at the controls, wearing sunglasses and a windcheater, had hair so pistol black it had to be fake. The boat crossed the river, leaving a high wake. Made a slow wide turn and came back, passing our moorings on his port side. The red-headed girl from the garden was standing next to the man, leaning into him as he pointed to different places on the island, her hair a red flag in the wind they made. The man seemed to be pointing directly at John and I, as we stood carefully balanced on the narrow roof of the barge.

I worried that their wash would knock us down if they came any closer.

Alex Kaplan, he said.

Trouble? I said.

Could be, John said.

That the girl? I said.

Alexandra, John said. Yes. But grown.

Somebody tell Gene?

Never pat a burning dog, the old man said.

Kaplan's boat sped past pirate flags newly raised, and hand-made posters protesting the fee increase. The signs were stuck to sides of boats, trees, wood pylons. All faced the river. Flyers were stuck to the fence surrounding the boatyard as though a great force had passed through the chain-link mesh and iron pickets leaving only these scraps of protest behind.

We watched the large white boat move upstream and out of sight.

Come on, John said.

Together we folded back the heavy canvas. Blackness gave way to bright colour under my feet. The red white and blue paintwork and signwriting John and Vesna had spent years restoring slowly revealed. The boat shone with the thickness of the paint. The many layers applied.

When I climbed down off the boat I could see it all.

Huge white letters on a white outlined red panel against the blue paint of the cabin. Grand Union Canal Carrying Company Co Ltd.

Black outline giving the letters a strong three-dimensional look. Real pop and impact. Underneath the company name was painted the address: Port of London EC3. A smaller red panel painted around a porthole gave the boat's name as *Vesna*.

Just below the roof a strip of white signwriting on a black panel declared that the boat had been registered at

Rickmansworth. Running the full length of the boat the gunwales were decorated with roses and diamond patterns of red white and blue. The two lower wood panels on the inside of each cabin door had been painted with pink, yellow and red roses on a dark-green, red-framed background. The upper panels each had a painting of a castle near water, the sea maybe, and under a bright blue sky.

There were two water cans painted in the same red white and blue colour scheme as the boat.

She was a wreck when we bought her, John said from the top of the boat.

I saw huge and steady tow-horses pulling the barges, carrying coal and iron castings from foundries. Heard the heavy steady clop of the horses, saw bargemen drinking in cutside pubs. Big horses tied to hitching posts with feed and water. Salt froth wiped away by the barge boy. Harnesses ornamented with brass put out to air, steaming.

More brightly decorated narrowboats and barges emerged from under winter covering. Stella's barge was painted navy and gold, and was decorated with birds, and images of the moon and stars. There were boats decorated with river scenes, with portraits of family members, dogs, regimental decals. Bands of coloured ribbon flew from the wheelhouse of an otherwise derelict tug. My own boat remained as it had been.

How was your winter?

A reed-like man materialized by my side. The drink on him like a vapour. Dirty, shoulder-length black hair showing some grey. Gold sleepers in his ears. Plain grey waistcoat over a white collarless shirt, thick, dark green corduroys, long white neckerchief loosely tied. Looked like some seventies rocker retired to the country. His shirt was frayed, the neckerchief stained with what could have been blood. Carried a big cloth bag that looked almost empty, the handles twisted around his hand, but I could make out bottles inside.

Tuppy Lawrence, he said.

Looking around at all the revealed boats.

Happy New Year, he said.

Could have been forty. Could have been older than me. Tuppy reached down and opened up the bag.

You're a drinking man, he said, a liquid catch at the back of his throat. The alcohol in the remaining bottles was almost clear, faintly blue.

The old man was looking down from the colourful sculpture of his boat, his long shadow on the path. The lightness of the sky behind him meant that there was no expression on his face that I could see.

The bootlegger closed the bag, looked over his shoulder. Turned back to me. The thin man's eyes were dirty yellow.

Hadn't brought so much as a tin of beer from Anthony Waters.

Not anymore, I said.

Tuppy nodded, smoothed his dirty neckerchief, glanced left and right at the decorated boats.

Good luck to you, he said.

White spit had collected at the corners of his mouth.

Without looking at me again he moved away along the tow-path. In the golden air of the summer afternoon the painted boats were new colour everywhere.

I thought of galas and harvest time. Carnivals. Country shows. Painted trucks, the stalls and rides and carousels. Street parties. Jack in the green. May fairs and May days. The light from the stained-glass windows in the church where I'd said goodbye to Nan.

Stella, a thin brush in one hand, a small tin of silver paint in the other, was kneeling on her deck repainting the face of the moon. She had an even thinner brush between her teeth. The deerhound stood guard while the boy was not to be seen. I made a fuss of the big grey dog.

Terry, Stella said, and smiled, and the little brush fell softly from her mouth into her open hand. When she caught the paintbrush that had, I'm certain, been forgotten in her mouth, this small magical act made her smile like a girl with no worries and no past.

She laid the paintbrushes down on the deck, began to stand and then had to reach for the brushes to stop them rolling away. She angled the brushes against each other so they'd stay where they were, stood up again, stretched. Rubbed the back of her neck, her hand paint-stained, navy and silver, fair hair escaping from the tight plait she'd put it in. The grey dog watched her all the time, and stretched when she did.

You want to help? Stella said.

I'd been drawing since I came to the island but I hadn't painted anything in months. I picked up the paintbrushes. Slender and electric in my hand.

Sure, I said.

Adam lugged the big piece of board down from the forest, carrying it above his head. Tall as me and twice as wide. Propped it on deck.

You wanted this? he said.

Gave him a fiver for it. Fair.

A bloody fiver, Adam said.

Kettle's boiled, I said.

Biscuits?

No biscuits.

The paint bubbled and was flaked from its long abandonment outside. But it was good for what I wanted it for.

In the first clear days of summer the three-arched bridge with its moving belt of colour was always there.

Drinking tea, Adam said: Won't be around for a few days. Me and Gene. Bit of work.

Doing what?

Demolition, he said. Rock breaking.

Gene say anything to you? I said. About the girl?

Gene's in his own world, the young giant said.

John came across from his boat to look at the big board.

What are you going to do with that? he said.

Nothing until it's bone dry, I said.

Nothing on a boat is ever bone dry, John said, haven't you learned that yet?

Adam and I carried the board into the sun-filled wheelhouse.

Come on, Adam said from the other end, horse it in there.

Stood the board up. Left it. Things to do.

Not washed my bedding all winter. Soaked the sheets and pillow in a bucket and put them out on deck to dry. Aired the thick blankets and then stowed them away. Swept out and cleaned the woodstove, opened the portholes and cleared the boat of leaves, berry juice and bird shit. Wiped down and polished the woodwork inside. At low tide I borrowed a long-handled brush from John and cleaned the green scum line on the hull knowing it would only come back in time. Even collected some wild forest flowers and put them in an empty coffee jar.

Borrow your stripper? I said to John.

What's that you say?

Your blower. Borrow it?

Didn't take all the old paint off. Wanted a rough surface though why was not a conscious thought.

A day's work, board was ready.

Had an old metal box of materials. Rabbit-skin glue was dried out, ruined. There was a palette knife. The last good brushes. Some paints but not much.

A cache of old letters from Evelyn Crow, full of praise, promises.

A man patting a good dog on the head.

Never mentioned exact figures.

A long, handwritten note. Called it une lettre privée.

'... you have had to invent for yourself the idea that you are an outcast. This has put more power into your elbow. And indeed it is an immensely sustaining thought for anybody ...'

When will I be done keeping this fist clenched in my chest my throat my skull?

Crow wanted me to paint what he told me to paint.

Who else believed in you?

I laid the board flat on the deck, and covered the lunar surface with a grey wash of varied thickness. Working fast. I thought about nothing but I saw Michael.

Said to Danny, who was on the deck, watching, white-haired, monkey-faced:

I'm trying to make exactly what I saw when I first came here and looked at the bridge. So that I can feel what I felt then.

As though instructed I painted the floating ovals that were what I saw when I looked downstream, halved in darkness and light.

Nicked Danny's pastels to make the sequence of moving coloured marks that were so important.

Hey! Danny said. Those are mine!

I went searching in the river mud at low tide. A copper coin worn smooth and aqua green. I couldn't date it or say what it had been worth. A knife blade or part of a blade, not red with rust as I would expect but midnight blue. Pieces of painted tile.

Stuck these finds on the canvas where it seemed indicated. With a palette knife applied a thick layer of transparent but sparkling acrylic gel. The river.

When it was finished the painting seemed to contain shifting, reflective movement, though maybe that belonged to the place it was made in, the June light, the water, the moving deck of the boat. What's the use of talking about it?

Aren't you worried? Danny said.

Danny was one of those evenly proportioned kids whose clothes, new or second-hand, clean or dirty, seemed made for him. I was watching him while Stella was at work. School was all right because there was a bus to take him, and she was usually home to meet him. Summer holidays, Stella told me, kids ran free and everybody, pretty much, watched over the kids. It was when the routine got disrupted for any reason that Stella asked for my help. The boy did not spend any nights away from the island, as far as I could tell.

About what?

Mum said we might have to leave.

The boy reached for the wolf mask. I'd never heard Stella talk about Danny's father. Nor the boy, and I wondered if he'd been told not to. The boy was holding it all in, his dad, all the things he'd seen and couldn't talk about. I thought he was a lot smarter than he let on, but I knew nothing about kids. And when I was a kid myself, men were absent or silent, violent or abusive. No exceptions. I said what we both expected me to say.

I'm sure it'll be all right.

I can't spare any paint, Stella had said when I'd asked her. We need it.

I thought we'd done the paintwork, I said.

The paint's for the posters. Against the rent increase, she said.

I'll trade you then.

You've got nothing to trade.

I'll watch Danny.

You do already.

Let me have some paint for my picture, I said, and I'll help with the posters. Come on, Stella.

It doesn't look like the river and the bridge, Danny said, looking at my painting, but it looks like the river and the bridge.

Mate, I said, you're an art critic.

Where are the people? the boy said.

You want your own board, I said. That it? What about this?

Lifted the board and turned it over.

A poster. The island seen from the river. Straight and tall trees with lush green tops. Painted and decorated boats looking like fairground rides. People doing things. Simple figures coiling ropes, washing decks, playing with dogs. I'd put Danny and the dog on the foreshore, the boy sun-blushed and ice cream-headed.

Thought about being with Nan when I was painting it.

We'd been somewhere – can't remember where – because we were in a railway station tearoom, and we were going home. Nan still herself, me small. Beeswax. Tea in a pot. Sit up nicely, Terry. A window box of *Dianthus* flowers – what Nan called pinks. Behind Nan's head a poster. Southern Railway. Beach scene. Golden child playing with a yellow dog on the sand. Blue sea.

I put black letters over the happy picture. Letters thick and hard-looking as prison bars. Read them from a mile off. Save our island.

What do you reckon? I said to Danny.

It's cool, Danny said.

Think your mum will like it?

She'll love it!

She did like it. Smiled when I handed it over. When she saw there was a painting on the other side, she looked at me in a different way than before.

You hear anything yet? Stella said. From Mrs Whitehead?

No, I said, she must still be overseas.

The dog wandered into view.

Shit.

John!

Bloody dog was covered in paint.

Stella laughed. Danny was curled up on my deck, crying he was laughing so hard.

Did you know she was there? I said. Did you paint her?

The boy couldn't answer. The painted dog was trying to lick the tears from the boy's face and he was laughing all the time.

What do you think you're doing boy? John shouted. Who told you to paint my dog?

Had the letter from Mrs Whitehead for a few days. Anthony watched my face when he handed it to me. Don't know why I didn't tell Stella. Made no difference. I couldn't afford to pay more, and there was nowhere else to go.

John couldn't stand the seabirds shitting on his bright paint-work. The gulls that came upriver were large, heavy birds. Big thump when they landed on your boat. The birds stomped around and left shit everywhere. Real brutes, with ugly pink feet they used to grab any bream or perch that came too close to the surface. John kept up a vigil.

Wore a carpenter's tool belt fitted out with cleaning materials that doubled up as weapons to use against the birds. A water spray that the old man would fire at the gulls to keep them off, or to clear away any shit that made it through his defences. The old man had different kinds of cloths for glass or paintwork, little tins and tubes of polishes, and he spent hours of every day trying to keep *Vesna* clean. Bird shit that he hadn't spotted, and that had hardened to the paint-work, enraged him. Wrapped the edge of a long handled chisel with gaffer tape so that he didn't mark the boat when he scraped off the shit. Watching birds congregated over and on the boat, and John would wave at them blindly with his chisel. There was one huge, smug-looking and malevo-lent bird who seemed to take pleasure in dive-bombing John, raining shit, then backing up just out of range.

The old man never got close to the gull but never stopped trying.

—

Summer. More and more strangers on the island. Friday night they'd come. A screen of yachts and cruisers tied alongside our boats, an hallucinated white mass. Late-night parties. Raised unfamiliar voices. I wouldn't have been able to describe an individual.

John's dog began to look to me if not for instruction then for company. What she didn't like were the seabirds. Kept out of their way. One night she stayed on my boat and puked and shat everywhere.

Something she'd eaten. Dead animal. Stink woke me up. Cleaned up the boat best as I could. Nearly puked myself.

Fuck's sake!

Shouting at the dog. She backed away like I was going to hit her. Shivering. Had to talk to her a long time before she'd come back to me.

Hey, I said, it's all right sweetheart. I'm sorry.

The dog had chunks of puke and smeared shit in her fur. I stank too. Refused to get in the small shower with me. I picked her up, my back screaming. She was scared and ashamed, and trembled in my arms. Panting from deep in her chest.

It's all right, I said, it's all right sweetheart.

Bright moon on the foreshore. Waded into the river, carrying the dog. She kicked against me but I held on tight. The water was freezing and shining black. The muddy river bottom sucked at my feet and threatened to unbalance me. I sang softly to her. When the water was above my waist I let her go. We swam, our heads above the water. The dog swam with her head back, her dilated eyes fixed on me. She swam in a wide loop and returned, her wake a shining circle under the moon. Claws scratching and leaving marks that were sore for days when she climbed back into my arms. Together we went to bed wrapped in all the blankets I could find. I heard her dreaming in the night.

When are you going to give this dog a name? John had said.

How's that my job?

I don't have time to be thinking up names for a blessed dog, John said.

She loved to sunbathe. Pouring bonelessly past me in the early mornings as I danced in the wheelhouse. Fitting herself to the angled plane of sunlit floor. Moving as she needed to stay in the light and warmth. She'd be on the floor before I got the door fully open. Stretching out the length of herself, pushing out her straightened legs and smacking her lips.

I kept a bowl filled with water on the boat at all times.

So Sunny maybe.

Don't give the dog a bad name, John had said.

In the light she was red really, and I took to calling her Red. Privately at first and then out loud, because I had to call her something. It was a name for a dog in a kids book, for a too good to be true dog.

In the forest she ran with light-footed, pitter-patter steps, her ears back and down, white-tipped tail held between her hind legs. Holding herself low to the ground, as though she were permanently ducking under a three-bar gate. Run ahead, turn and lie down with her head between her white socks, eyes fixed on me until I reached her, and then she'd take off again.

She would try and work any group of standing crows. Blocking their escape except for the direction she wanted to move in. The crows hopping away sideways. Red circling, pushing them where she wanted them to go until she had sufficiently annoyed the birds into flight. Many of the crows looked a bit rough-faced and battered from their war with the parakeets for nesting spaces and food.

Red panting in the heat. The valleyed tongue hanging down. Wet and thick. Still she worked the phantom stock. Driving ghost sheep, a retinue of insects fizzing in the light that surrounded her. Slobber darkening the ground in repeated patterns.

Joined at the hip, Adam said, when we came into the camp.

Parakeets in the treetops made a jungle din.

Red let Adam rough her up with his big hands. When he was finished she stood up and shook herself, one ear turned inside out, a little dazed, her coat dusted with seeds and stalks and dry earth. The mother dog stood up. Black and white. A bit woolly looking. She stretched and walked over to Adam. The big youth blew on her snout and she loudly snapped her jaws at him. Adam got on the ground and they started wrestling.

Adam dusted himself off and went into his shelter, the mother dog following. When they came out Adam was carrying a huge bag of dry food under one arm and a big metal bowl in the other. The dog had her head raised to the bag of food. What looked like a soup ladle was sticking out the back pocket of Adam's work trousers. Adam banged the ladle against the metal bowl. The ringing echoed through the forest.

The dogs loped in to the camp like cowboys called for breakfast, Red leading the way. Adam fed the dogs, talking to them, his hands always making contact. The dogs ate from the communal bowl and when they were finished Adam filled the bowl with water and the dogs drank noisily. Splashed water made a dark circle on the ground.

You love it here, I said.

Don't like being inside, he said, and scratched his arm and looked at the ground where the dogs were now lying down, bellies swollen with food and water.

Ha!

Simple as that, I said.

Adam held his hands cupped at waist level and looked at me.

When my mum and dad went on the piss, he said, they'd lock me in my room with some biscuits and maybe a Fanta, a Coke. Sometimes dad would forget the drink, so I couldn't eat the biscuits. Got too thirsty. But I'd eat them in the end. If I was there long enough. Course then I'd get so thirsty I thought I'd go crazy. Do anything. Tried drinking my piss once.

The dogs dreamed. You had to listen if you wanted to hear the quiet sounds that came to us in the clearing. Not just the birds but the soft air making the leaves rattle. Water noises.

Adam took the offered roll-up. Green eyes shining from out of his scarred face.

No toilet in there, Adam said. Had to go in a corner. Shit too. Summer. Imagine. Days sometimes. I used to see how long I could last and still hope they wouldn't come back.

Smash a window? I said. Get help?

Thought it were normal, Adam said, his eyes wide. Thought every kid got locked up.

How'd you get away?

Dad picked a fight with the wrong blokes. Tough town. Squaddies. Multiple stab wounds. Came to tell mum, arrested her instead. Took me away. Made Old Bill sick when they found me and saw the room I was in.

A magpie flew into the camp, making short, clacky calls. I looked for its mate.

Adam opened his large, heavy hands and looked at them. When they took me from that room, he said. I thought I was saved. Little did I know. Hah! Every room they put me into afterwards, they locked me in!

What happened?

In the end? I got big. Big so they couldn't hold me. Fucked off. Here I am. If they could see me now, he said, and laughed and spread his arms.

The dogs came into his embrace.

Adam looked at me.

My old man never even tried to get sober, he said. Swore up and down he would, but he never tried.

Don't make me out to be anything, I said. The last bender I went on lasted twenty years and nearly killed me. I wouldn't survive another one.

Lights still shining on John's boat when I finally made it back. I called out, knocked on the cabin door with the flat of my hand.

You did not walk onto a boat uninvited without good reason and never at night.

Not twice, John said.

The old man had a ten-pound lump hammer behind his cabin door.

Never used it and don't expect to use it, he'd said. Not with the dog here now. But you never know.

John had lots of reasons to sit up nights.

Two ships torpedoed out from under him during the war. Spent a night and a day up to his chest in the bone-cold Atlantic. Fuel burning all around.

Planes firing at us from above, he said. Men screaming, on fire, going under. Sharks and who knows what below.

The old man was holding an ancient-looking scuffed tennis ball.

Where's the dog? he said.

She's here, I said. Go on Red.

The dog jumped up on the sofa and nuzzled into John.

He chucked the dog under the chin and ruffled her ears.

If I drop the case, John said, my lawyer says they'll give me money.

Who, I said, the care home?

They call it compensation. Blood money. They want to buy my right to vengeance.

How much? I said.

Enough to stay here, John said.

That's good, isn't it? I said.

A thump as a bird landed on the boat. John threw the tennis ball underhand but hard at the ceiling and caught it as it bounced and came down. Red's head going up and down as she followed the ball. I looked at the photographs, the records and books. One missed catch and there would be damage and the dog going wild but John Rose believed in himself and what he was doing.

What do you know about loving somebody? the old man had said when I asked him what he was going to do. I sat in the wheelhouse with just the moon for light and I couldn't think of an answer though the boat seemed empty with Red not there.

The pale places in the sky grew larger, and the wide river appeared out of the dark, soft grey at first, then shining to reflect the rising sun. Fragile colours blooming so that the dog and I, standing in the bow, in the join between sky and river, were bathed in immense peach and golden washes. The sunrise and the image of the sunrise. Sounds – waking voices, birdsong, the indefinite, mysterious sounds made by creatures who lived on or under the water – all these echoed across the river. Softly we were reached by the edges of the hot day to come. The river becoming a dazzling plain on which the floating bridge seemed a mirage.

Come on, I said to Red.

Lush elderflower along the riverbank.

In the forest by Michael's stones I found a new young tree, grown from a whip or unbranched shoot. A disc on the tree identified it as a Western cedar.

The forest green. Following the dog, the low sun showing through different trees made the ground cover a shifting iridescence, hazy with flying insects. I thought I heard grasshoppers. Treetops moved against each other making a sound like surf.

The light directed just so to reveal the small tree otherwise invisible against its giant neighbours.

A ceramic heart. 'MV + AK'.

When crushed, the leaves of the Western cedar have a scent like pineapples.

Way above me, in that small measure of it I could see between the swaying treetops, wheeling crows cut slow black patterns in the sky. An arrow whizzed past my head. Red barked.

I whirled round. The kids were up with the sun.

Danny and his friends hunted each other among the trees near the water. Bows made from cut lengths of PVC piping. Tight string keeping the piping arced. Arrows made from sticks, young tree stems, found bamboo, anything that would fly, the heads softened with felt pads. Danny fired another arrow that bopped against my heart. I fell to the ground with a great death yell that scared Red.

I am des-troyed! I cried, Is zis ze end for Terry Black-heart, ze legendary French trapper?

Mum says come and have something to eat later, the boy said, standing over me with a padded arrow in his hand, his white hair falling into his face. Not dirty so much as wearing the marks and signs of the outside places – the forest and the muddy foreshore – where he spent all his time. Clothes worn yesterday and tomorrow. Jeans that stood up by themselves, a second skin.

The raiding party moved on. I had seen them firing their arrows uselessly at the big white launches and cruises that, more and more, were seen on our stretch of river.

Red licked the hand that smelled of pineapples.

—

Spent the day making designs for posters and flyers. When John came back from wherever he'd been, tired, not speaking, he took the dog with him, and I went to Stella's barge.

There was an open porthole above the stove and Stella's face, turned to me when she spoke, was lit pale honey by that small portion of a summer's evening the opening allowed to enter, so that the skin on her face was both a radiant and reflective surface, lined around her grey-blue eyes. Wheat coloured hair piled and tied loosely on the top of her head. The curved nose and thin lips that gave a suggestion of a bird, so light that you only thought about it when she was gone, and trying to remember what she looked like.

Choo-Choo the deerhound lay on the floor next to Danny. Now and again the boy absently curled one of the dog's ears around his finger. First one then the other. Couldn't bring Red over because the long grey dog would go mad.

Stella was wearing a grey sweatshirt that was too big and she had to keep pushing the sleeves up her arms and out of the cooking pot. The sweatshirt would fit somebody twice her size. Black combat trousers and black polyurethane clogs. She wore a Casio digital watch, and old-looking gold earrings and a gold chain that she had told me belonged to her grandmother.

For dinner there was veggie curry and rice. We ate and afterwards I washed up and Danny helped me dry the dishes. Stella and Danny disappeared for a bit while she put him to bed. I sat with the deerhound's head in my lap.

Choo-Choo, Stella said.

The dog unfolded, stood, shook itself, and followed us up top.

We sat under red clouds, in the navy folds of river and sky.

The boats all around variously dark or lighted. The differently shaped roofs. Flat, pitched, wide, narrow.

Radios playing. People talking. The sound of water endlessly moving. Meeting solid matter, the hulls and sides of boats, and being interrupted by that. Glop. Night bird sounds. The skating whoosh of a swan landing on water.

Stella took the cigarette from my mouth, took a puff and put it back.

The grey deerhound flew across the boats and jumped down onto the island. She disappeared into the darkness.

Can you tell me about the wolf mask? I said.

Stella looked at me. Took the cigarette back and smoked until it was finished.

Kids don't want to be different, she said. It was a tough few months for Danny before we came here. Top of that he has to start a new school. Some kids started on Danny. Names. Feral. Must have heard the word somewhere. Parents. Danny doesn't know what it means. But he doesn't say anything. Doesn't want to worry me. Tells Michael, and Michael brings him the wolf mask. God knows where he got it from.

Feral means wild, Michael tells Danny. Free. Escaped. Bears are feral. Lions and tigers. Everything that lives in the forest and the river. The finches and blue tits and robins that come when it's time for spring.

Michael was what, fifteen. Then he gives him the mask. Wolves are feral, he says.

Feral meant gone wild, as far as I knew. So Michael was wrong but he was right, too.

Must be tough for Danny, I said, now.

It's tough to keep losing, she said.

When we came here, she said, I left a lot of debt behind. Left Danny's dad, tried to make a life. Get all the things for Danny. Place to live. The phones, the screens, the games. Got swallowed up. Had to run or lose my son.

All right.

Stella's not even my real name.

My ex is dangerous, she said.

She rolled her sleeve up past her elbow and I could see an old break, where the skin was not smooth but almost violet and tightly swollen over a bone that had been left to heal by itself and not set properly.

Never heard the word no in his life, she said.

What did you do, before?

Human resources, she said. I was an office manager. Danny's father was my boss. He beat me, whored around. For years.

Go to the cops?

Richard plays golf with the police, she said. So we ran. You're Danny, I told him. Day one. Don't answer to anything else. Don't answer the phone unless it's me. Don't let anybody in. Call me mum or Stella. Danny wasn't even ten. He goes, OK Stella, just like that.

Seen the new tree, I said, by the stones?

She hadn't, too busy, so I told her.

Good for her I say, said Stella.

Alexandra?

I've never believed in any conspiracy, she said. It was just a terrible accident. Awful for Alexandra, what was she, sixteen? A baby. Alex Kaplan got her out because he could. Did what a father should. The kids were sweethearts, for God's sake. Poor girl was probably traumatized. Nobody's seriously suggesting she had anything to do with what happened.

Not even Gene? I said.

Poor Gene, she said. He's heartbroken. Couldn't do what Kaplan did. Protect his child. The police won't leave him alone. Angry because he's full of love. You never saw him before.

Gene's got Perseis, I said.

The skin around Stella's neck flushed pink.

Perseis walks around feeling sorry for herself, she said. She did that even when Michael was alive. God, I sound like a real bitch. But she never listened to Michael.

Perseis had come to my boat a day or so before with an invitation, a crown of wildflowers in her short dark hair. Wearing a green tabard dress tied at the waist with a golden cord that trailed almost to the ground, and square-toed scuffed boots. Going from boat to boat, handing out cards. Her progress set the boats see-sawing. She was high, protected for as long as that lasted. She said my name as though she thought I'd been waiting a long time to see her. Maybe it's also true that for her the world was a place filled with people who would not look her in the eye.

A fast boat roared downstream, its fringing wake high and wide.

Before Michael went away Anthony used to take him all up and down this river, she said.

Anthony Waters? I said.

Anthony would do anything for me, she said.

Perseis played with the golden cord. She put the cord in her lap and felt the cut end, then brushed it against her palm.

When she looked at me directly she seemed to see something only she could see, hear sounds only she could hear. I could smell her. The funk of her. Thick and coppery like blood and salty like tears. I could smell her but I'm not sure she was there. She was with Michael, I think. I expect she always was. How she imagined it would be. Maybe she and her son were with Anthony Waters. Putting things right that never could be put right.

I took one of the printed cards. A wood engraving. Forest interior characterized by depth and texture and a clear sense of pattern. Ducking my eye under low dark ash branches to get to the lighted clearing beyond. Crude only because the maker did not have access to proper engraving tools but had improvised with who knows what to gouge and cut the lines.

Celebrating Michael Vincent on the back. Date and time.

We'll do this every year, she said. A coming together. To

remember Michael and hope for his return. Anthony was very good to have the cards printed.

I realized that Gene had probably been called Gene from boyhood, and was not his real name.

I'm a little scared of John Rose, she said, giving me another invitation. Would you mind?

I took the extra card. Far as I could tell John didn't like her. A damned hippy with ideas. John would look at her and see nothing but bad news and worse memories. I thought all this without knowing a single thing about what happened. I was some detective.

We went back below. Danny has bad dreams, Stella had said.

How was the meeting? I said.

A lot of anger. Can't pay, won't pay. I don't think Kaplan's a monster but what he's planning will ruin lives and destroy this community. The resistance is strong.

What if you have to leave? I said.

Where to?

Somewhere else.

There isn't anywhere else, Stella said.

Stella pushed up the sleeves of the too-big sweatshirt.

All I had to do was kiss her.

Whenever the tide changed, you could feel the heavy bulk of water pulling underneath your feet. I could feel it now. Leaning almost to hold my stance. Slack ropes tightening. I could hear fenders groaning as the bound houseboats were subject to the change in the volume and direction of water.

As though we were slowly being pulled loose. The boat and the three of us and the deerhound, asleep again now, and the jars of sumac and mint and nettle seeds on Stella's shelves, Danny's open box of crayons and coloured pencils, the painted jug full of sweet peas and forget-me-nots. The home-made red-and-white checkered curtains. I straightened a ladle and then a metal spoon hanging on hooks by the stove, and when I let go the ladle and spoon swung a few degrees towards upstream.

She'd given me no sign.

I should be going, I said. Thanks for dinner.

Thanks for the help, she said.

Anytime.

Red stood in the river up to her rusty flanks, barking with happiness. Jaws dripping water, bright teeth sharp, looming over the fleet of model boats at the water's edge. Summer solstice. A black flag with a luminous skull and crossbones was raised over the island.

More flags and banners flew from boats, from the trees, from the weir's iron bridge. John Rose's narrowboat showed a faded red ensign. Protest flags, black flags, golden flags like tall curved sails, flags embroidered or painted with words and symbols: anarchist signs, peace signs, rainbows, No Evictions, Save Our Boats.

Gene had asked me to help him make a flag for Michael.

Make it big, Gene said, and I did, working bare-chested through a hot afternoon, painting Michael's face on a sheet in bold and large black lines. The lost boy's banner flew below the skull and crossbones. Like something you see at the football. The kid even looked a bit like Maradona. Gene watching over me, his shadow falling on the work, becoming bigger as the sun moved. Finally had to ask him to move. Still feel the sunburn on my shoulders.

All right? I'd said when it was finished.

Gene gently put his hand on my already sore shoulder.

Yes mate, he'd said. Lovely.

—

Little kids, bloody and mutilated, with stuck-on beards and wooden swords edged with silver foil, ran laughing and yelling along the shoreline. Adam running with them, a laughing kid under each arm, another on the youth's huge back.

Smoke rose from cooking fires, blue smoke into blue. The island buzzing with talk, shouts, laughter, overlapping music and happy dogs.

The slender bootlegger Tuppy Lawrence, dressed like a castaway in torn clothes, carried an open boat carved from styrofoam down to the shoreline. A lone plasticine figure aboard, mad-eyed, in rags, a kicked-over empty water barrel by his bare feet, surrounded by the bones and half-eaten bodies of ships' officers, who lay dead among torn sashes and scraps of golden braid.

Tuppy's lifeboat was mounted on a styrofoam base, painted like a rough sea, crowded with the surfacing fins and wide open jaws of frenzied sharks. The boat and figure were glazed with sealant of some kind but which seemed flavoured with petrol. The warm summer air was thick with accelerant.

Every kind of boat crowded the shore, dust rags and patches of faded denim for sails. Masts made from chopsticks, big kitchen matches, tree sprigs. There were cardboard barges, a couple of friendly tugs. Found materials, saved and salvaged. The fruits of expert mudlarking.

Different boats fell into stormy shadows as Red splashed through the water. The dog huffed at the bloody castaway, her head like a huge triangular storm cloud passing over the lifeboat.

Stella and Danny held aloft a ship of the line with matchstick-firing cannons.

A cardboard trawler's tinfoil hold brimmed with a catch, the fish made by multi-coloured match heads dusted with glitter. Figures painted yellow to make sou'westers pulling hard to raise another net.

John Rose carried a large cruise ship or passenger liner to the water's edge. The ship's many windows were made from what may have been plastic film stock, or the glassine windows of unpaid bills. Crowded at the rails and looking out from the windows were many black figures, in hats and suits and best dresses. Toy soldiers John had disarmed and repainted as civilians, the costumes cut from coloured paper. The ship's two funnels, made from plastic coffee cups salvaged from the river, were lined with nests of wire mesh packed with wood shavings and scraps of newspaper.

Gene carried a red sailboat.

How long had everybody been busy making their boats in secret?

Two cops had been with us all day. Young and younger. Tall and short. The close-cut barnets. Wrap-around sunglasses. The thick-soled shoes. Making it clear. No body found. Case still open.

Shadowing Gene. Who was a fist. Closed and hard.

Perseis wore a different wildflower crown, and I had a vision of her in the dark, candlelit barge, fixing dead flowers and grasses to rings of wire.

Now there were long shadows on the ground. A big sky patterned with the last of the sun's fiery light.

We sat under paper lanterns while John showed a pieced-together home movie on a rigged-up screen made by a sheet between two trees.

A young, black-haired woman in a flowered headscarf at the wheel of a moving boat that looked familiar until I realized it was my boat, before the superstructure of the wheelhouse was added. The woman – Mrs Whitehead? – waved at the person holding the camera – John or Vesna, it had to be – before the barge chugged past and the woman and her flowery headscarf slowly vanished, the silver river the last image to disappear, and then that section of film ended.

Now here came *Vesna* unrestored, sorry-looking were it not for the boat's jaunty progress on the water, and her smart ensign. A younger John at the wheel in a blue cap and startlingly bright red jumper, grinning like a settler in a new world, haloed by a dense cloud of diesel exhaust.

Something about the film used – was it Technicolor? – the bright sheet it was projected onto or the lantern light we watched it in, sharpened all the primary colours, so that John in his red sweater seemed a vital presence, a world-builder.

Thirty seconds of Perseis holding a baby, Michael, and sitting on the bench seat of a dinghy next to a smiling blonde woman I knew to be Vesna. Perseis softer, in a T-shirt and denim shorts, her dark hair not cropped down but falling past her shoulders. Both women blushed with sunshine, Michael grabbing at the spangles of light dancing on the water surrounding the boat, his little hand opening and closing.

Then Michael with chubby legs, launching a sailboat onto the water, the fingers of a big disembodied hand, Gene's hand, holding the child safe at the water's edge.

The shadows or outlines of islanders passed in front and behind the sheet that sometimes lifted or otherwise moved on the summer breeze, these present images joining with footage of Michael and Danny ('Hey, that's me!') playing in the fractured light of a clearing in the forest.

And then Gene's image suddenly, looking so completely changed I thought at first it might be somebody I didn't know, who looked a bit like Gene but whose face was smooth, whose large clear eyes were radiant with happiness and belonging, and whose head was untouched by the shroud of grey that covered it now. Gene was black-haired in this incarnation, like Michael, curly heads both, and you could see how strongly the boy took after his dad. Wiry, big-eyed. Sitting either side of Perseis, who laughed and made a face, crossing her eyes and blowing her cheeks out, then laughed again and tucked a long strand of her hair back behind her ear. The family all holding gold ice-cream wafers.

A woman, Perseis, cried out.

Gene's voice calling from the darkness:

Why don't you turn that fucking thing off, John?

The film stopped, the sheet becoming blank, and I could hear the sound of a motorboat, quiet and then loud, moving fast. Both men were staring at the empty space where their younger selves, and the ghosts of the people they had loved the most, had moved again in the sunshine of the past. Stella was holding Perseis and talking to her.

John Rose said something to Gene I couldn't hear, and Gene nodded, at least I think he did, and then he looked at the river, and moved towards the rising noise of an outboard engine.

Three figures in the boat speeding across the river towards us. Bright wake on the darkening water. Kaplan, at the wheel, in a black shirt and a windbreaker, the material shiny like a heat blanket, the tall, red-haired girl, and sitting close to the girl Anthony Waters, also in black. All wearing sunglasses against the wind and spray.

When Waters led the girl onto the island there was no sign of Alex Kaplan.

The air was thick with heat and unburned fuel. The longest day finally turned to evening.

Poor Michael. A girl you'd make wild promises to you wouldn't be able to keep. She was taller than any of the people who were staring at her. Pale face pinned with thousands of freckles. The redness of her hair under a black bandeau fire behind a screen. She'd never be able to go anywhere without being noticed, but for two years nobody had remembered seeing her with Michael on the day he died.

The tall cop raised his phone to take a picture of her.

Angry looks thrown his way. A few shouts. Waters made

a movement towards the cop that was so slight I almost didn't see it.

The cop's partner said something from behind his hand, and the tall cop made a face and put his phone away. The short cop said something else, lifted his head towards Gene, and the tall cop nodded.

I hadn't seen where Waters came from and when he stepped away he disappeared from view, but I knew he was there. Knew he was watching as Gene, pulling Perseis by the hand, moved towards the girl. Hot breeze making the flags snap, and ruffling the fur of dogs.

Gene and the girl met each other and the girl reached for Gene's hands. Gene's death-white face tightened even more. The girl had her head bowed. Perseis looking at them both, her hands wringing out the golden cord. Gene and the girl held each other for a long time. I could hear the girl talking but not what she said. Gene swayed in the almost purple light.

John Rose was still standing in front of the white sheet, his form made dark, the sheet bordered by the leaves of the trees it had been roped between, a composition of man and sheet and green leaves. Not sure the old man had moved since Gene had spoken roughly to him.

Perseis made a noise like a growl. Waters appeared. Stood close behind her.

The girl put her red head against Gene's chest. They held each other. Finally Gene let the girl go. Said something to her I couldn't hear. She nodded. Wiped her face. Perseis stepped towards him and touched his sleeve. Gene pushed her hand away without looking at her.

Oh Gene, she cried.

Call the fucking divers, Steve! Gene shouted at the cops.

Perseis still pulling at his sleeve.

Told you! Gene shouted. Told everybody!

The tall cop took his hands out of his pockets, said something I couldn't hear. Pointed upwards, then rubbed his thumb and forefingers together, shook his head.

Fuck excuses, Steve, Gene said. Just get them in the water.

Perseis began to fall. Waters materialized once more. Caught her. Held her up. Made her look at him. Smiled. Pushed a non-existent curl of hair behind her ear.

Gene let him.

You were right, I heard her say.

She said it again, but I didn't know which of the two men she was talking to.

Waters put his arm around her and led her away.

When Waters sat down beside me much later, he was holding a half-empty bottle of red wine.

Drinking from a paper cup held inside another cup. Something different about him. The wine he'd drunk, or maybe it was just that I was looking at him more closely. There were two new security cameras in his shop, and two more on the top of the fence that surrounded the boatyard. The camera casings were a matt naval grey.

Sandy hair damped down and lightly scented with

something. The skin of his face was tight and so pink you might think he'd shaved twice. Changed his clothes. Short sleeve white shirt, biscuit-coloured slacks.

What are you, I said, an ex-cop?

Waters shrugged, drank some wine.

I was a soldier, he said. Then I went to work for Mr Kaplan, for whom I perform many duties. As you have seen.

Do you remember Brady Millar? I said.

A small smile.

Welterweight, he said. A very dangerous fighter. When active. A man with an education. Stood out.

You wouldn't know where he is?

Waters looked at me like he wanted to kick me down a flight of stairs. Colour flooded his face.

Why on earth would I know that?

You're Mr Kaplan's security man.

Was, and the Millar case was before my time.

All right, I said, but you must have an idea.

Waters put his cup of wine on the ground.

Looked at him. Light scar tissue around the eyes. Economy of movement. Skin of his hands smooth the way fighters' hands get sometimes.

I know you're Brady Millar, I said. I know that much. I just don't know what you're doing here.

This time he laughed out loud. But he wouldn't look at me.

Strange that he'd keep you around, I said. Must be something in it, but it makes no difference to me.

You don't know what you're talking about, he said.

Waters looked at me. No expression. Hard thin mouth full and violet with wine.

Mr Godden, Waters said finally, what you don't know about me and Mr Kaplan and this island would take too much explaining.

Try me, I said.

Mr Kaplan's changes will make this a better place.

Not for the people who are already here, I said. They can't afford to stay.

Some can, he said. People tell me things they wouldn't tell a stranger.

Why are you here, I said, really? Kaplan pay you off? What have you got on him?

Waters swirled the wine in the plastic cup. When he looked up he was smiling. Almost didn't recognize him.

I am persuaded to believe, he said at last, that my future is here.

The ex-soldier, maybe former boxer, stood straight up without any apparent effort. Still holding the wine bottle and the two plastic cups, he walked back towards the dark lines of boats.

Long ago, and as strong and wild as I was ever going to get, I met a rich, twenty-year-old Greek girl, who told me straight out that she'd sleep with me because it would piss off her dad. Flavia was looking for something I couldn't give her, even if she knew what it was. She was playing pool badly in a pub she shouldn't have been in, wearing a sheer silver dress with thin strips crossing the hollows of her collarbone, her anger a force field. The dress moving on her and with her.

Thick dirty-blonde hair chopped off at the neck. Face an oval, cheekbones you could cut a rope with. Straight nose and full lips. Dark eyes that told a different, sadder story about herself than any she told me.

Pub closed so taxi back to her place. Something Lodge. Modernist. Decorative concrete screens. We fell in the door. If I'd been her dad that's as far as I'd ever get, but he offered me a glass of pomegranate-coloured liquor I didn't recognize, and asked me what else I did when Flavia told him I was a painter.

For money, he said.

The bottle sat on a table that shone with inlaid coloured stones. Both of them looked like they would cost too much.

We're going up to my room, Flavia said.

Have you eaten? her father said. Darling?

Naked she was too slim, enough to worry me.

She did what she liked, she said what she liked. I was hooked. Crazy loud in bed, but not for my benefit. Later Adrian, her father, bought one of the full-length paintings I made of her.

Flavia showed me pictures of her dad's house on a Greek island. I forget the name. White house, red tiles, blue sea. Said we'd go there. We never did. Where I got the idea though. Get there some day. Place like that.

I hadn't thought about her in years. Flavia.

Tuppy was dead drunk, flat out near the water like a

sailor washed ashore. Red crept near to him but I called her away.

Adam, his face painted like one of his dogs, sat down beside me.

The girl told the police everything, he said. What she came home for. Said she saw Michael go into the river and never come out. That Steve cop said has Gene threatened you? She said Mr Vincent hasn't threatened me, no.

Poor Gene, I said.

You know how it is, the big youth said, looking at me with painted whiskers on his face and a black nose, the paint hiding his scars.

Gene, in his own world, waded into the water holding a burning torch high above his head. Brought the torch down and set the red sailboat on fire. Released it flaming onto the water, where air on the river filled the pure white sail. The feathery summer wind made little ridges and pleats on the water. You could see these in the light made by the waterborne candles, so that the impression was of light being thrown on soft turbulence. The candlelit water dirty brown.

The red sailboat drifted into a cardboard barge and it went up in flames. Another boat, a man-of-war, caught fire. Up to his waist in the river, Gene watched the boats burn, the reflection of the flames dancing on his pale, stricken face, the flames themselves visible on the surface of the water and in Gene's black eyes.

Small, quick fires. Torched fragments carried up into the

night sky in bursting flakes of red and gold. The smell of burning paper, wood, petrol. The boats that passed through the fires unharmed were lucky, or better built. Though the funnels smoked, John's liner remained somehow intact, moving with what seemed secret purpose towards midriver, out of my sight.

I thought of ships, of armies, hanging on.

There's a blessed porpoise in the river, John Rose said in the morning.

No sign of the coffee I was dying for.

Slept in his party clothes. Lilac-coloured open-neck shirt, with a violet neckerchief, white cord trousers and blue and white deck shoes. Everything not dirty and not clean. The outfit looked different in the morning, like he'd found and put on half-remembered clothes from the dressing-up box of somebody else's past.

Stale whisky on his breath. Ashy skin. Dirty-white crust at the corners of his mouth and his yellow eyes.

Looking a bit doolally.

You all right, John?

No answer. Gazing upstream, somewhere beyond the light blossoming in mysterious sequence on the water.

Vertical flags were shrouds hidden in the trees. The still air flavoured with dead fires, the made fleet vanished. A single wine bottle moving on the tide at the river's edge. The reed grass near the towpath was beaten down, burned-looking, lifeless.

But the peachy light made me giddy. Wanted to bite shapes out of it, grab it in handfuls.

Red barked on the foreshore, her front legs in the water, the fur along her back raised and spiked.

Terry, the old man said, can't you see?

Two jet-skis burst from under the willows, racing each other, huge spouts of water rising behind them, wet chainsaw sound ripping through the morning. Crows and parakeets came rushing up out of the forest into the high clear sky.

The dolphin surfaced under a coronet of expelled air. Breaking the skin between worlds. A single arc through the water. Shallow, fugitive. Then she was gone.

Whooping from the jet-skis. Higher revs. Machines gaining, roaring, petrol rainbows in the spray.

We watched, John from his boat, me from mine.

Red barking all the time and running up and back along the shoreline.

John cried out, hand shielding his eyes.

The dolphin surfaced again, far ahead, something mythical, glimpsed. Rising and disappearing in the same moment, jet-skis chasing. Almost impossible to have seen against the dark riverbank, except that John's old sailor eyes had seen.

The machine screamed past the dolphin, turning hard to cut the animal off. Made a tight half turn that became an out of control spiral when the engine failed. High fan of water following the boat's spin. The jet-ski tipped over on its side, the rider thrown off into the water.

The second jet-ski, with two figures riding her, revved down and turned back.

She'll likely die in the river, I said.

Yes, John said, but not because of those bastards.

The old man coughed and spat, the hollow of his throat moving up and down.

The jet-skiers came onto the island. Red heard them first. They must have brought the machines round and tied up at the boatyard. Big, healthy-looking kids with large white teeth and big feet. All three of them wearing long pastel shorts and polo shirts with the collars turned up. Pink, sky blue, orange. Sky-blue shirt wore a New York baseball cap.

The biggest kid was tying his wet blonde hair up in a bun.

Water dripped from his pink polo shirt and shorts.

The three of them slapping along in flip-flops with a little Brazilian flag on them. Big, hairy white toes hanging over the edge of the flip-flop. Made my stomach turn.

Red turning round in circles, barking all the time.

Get below Red, John said.

The dog looked outraged for a second, then sloped into the barge.

The blonde kid waved at John from up on the towpath.

We come in peace, he said.

Sky blue shirt sniggered.

Amazing boat, the kid in the orange shirt said. Really amazing. My dad keeps saying he's going to buy one of these. How much would something like this cost?

We're looking for Alex, the blonde kid said, when John didn't answer.

Alex Kaplan? I said, coming out of the open wheelhouse.

The blonde kid hadn't seen me. No time to set his face.

I'd seen the ugly look a million times.

Alexandra, the kid in the cap said. The exiled princess, back in town.

The kid looked John up and down, then turned his cap round so it sat backwards on his head. Crossed his arms over his chest. Made shapes with his fingers that I didn't understand.

Just think about that for a second, he said.

What the fuck Bruce, the third kid said.

This is her island right? the kid called Bruce said, playing with his cap. Alex's. So you have to tell us where she is, right. There must be a law or something.

Bruce, the third kid said, seriously.

Shut up Cooper.

Rage uncoiling inside me.

Red barked.

John went below.

A breeze from the river lifted the flags in the trees. The pirate flag, Michael's face, unfurled and became briefly visible. The boys looked up at the sound of the material snapping.

Whoa, the boy called Bruce said, did you see that Dex?

The blonde boy laughed and said something I didn't hear, but his friends laughed with him.

Kid's feet were almost level with my head. Could have reached out and grabbed his legs. Pulled him into the river.

Behind me something heavy was being dragged across a deck. John was standing on the tarpaulin-covered empty boat that was between his painted barge and my boat. Holding the lump hammer by the handle, down by his side.

Shooma alley come! John shouted. Shooma alley come!

Lifted the lump hammer and shook it at the kids.

The old man reached for the gunwale of my boat with his free hand. Dropped the heavy hammer onto the deck of the empty boat. Went down on one knee.

What the fuck? the boy in the cap said.

John! I shouted.

The old man's crazy, the blonde kid said. Let's get out of here. Come on!

Was a damn porpoise! John said later.

You seen many dolphins in the river? I'd asked him.

I wasn't going to argue with him.

We were in the wheelhouse. The evening sky was ruby and charcoal. Red had her head in the old man's lap, and John was pushing his large hand over her, going with the grain of Red's coat, flattening the dog's ears and making her eyes look wild and staring. Then he pushed the fur the other way so the fur stood up. Then he started again.

The old man looked better. Been to bed.

You had your dander up, I said. What were you shouting at those kids?

Aden, John said, his voice low, phlegmy.

Long time ago. Maybe sixty years. Shore leave. Got my pocket picked in the market. Run after this little youth. Wasn't going to catch him. Kid ran straight into this old man. The old man starts shaking and slapping him and really beating the youth. Pointing at the kid's skin and his own skin and then pointing at my skin and then whupping the boy around the head. All the time shouting: hshuma alaikum, hshuma alaikum.

What's it mean, John?

Shame on you, he said, I find that out. Shame on you in the name of God.

Red yawned. Keeping her head in John's lap she turned her body upside down.

You can't rely on them here, John said. Somewhere like Aden, they would lead the ship into port and lead her out again. So many you couldn't count them.

What's that?

Porpoises, he said.

Adam smoothed out a crushed piece of paper on the banquette. Ripped where he'd pulled the notice from the tree it was nailed to.

Take a look, he said.

Big meaty hands. He'd had the use of them, as Nan would have said.

The crumpled sheet and Adam's living hands looked like they wanted nothing to do with each other.

Didn't trust official letters. Told a story about your life you hadn't written. Didn't recognize. Subject to what the words said you were. Until you couldn't be seen for all the black bars of type. But paper in all forms was also the material I worked with. Many times I'd turned over official letters to make a drawing on the back. Every clean piece of paper was a magic carpet. Even the crushed sheet under my hand.

It was late. Still warm. New moon. The wheelhouse door was open, letting our smoke out and the night sounds in. Birds called to each other like fond comrades. Music pulsed across the dark river. Kaplan's house. A big party. All the lights burning.

Whirring moths crowded the wheelhouse bulb.

What's it say? Adam said.

Made the mistake of looking at him.

I can read, the young giant said, putting on a fierce face. Just not all the legal bollocks.

Course, I said. Who understands that? Different language. Pass me my glasses.

Adam handed me the glasses without looking at me.

Right, I said, and read the notice of eviction out loud.

To anybody living in the forest:

You are illegally squatting on private land. You will be given a generous amount of time to leave voluntarily, but if you have not dismantled the camp and left by August thirty-first, you will be forcibly evicted and charged with:

Causing damage while in the property.

Not leaving when they're told to by a court.

Stealing from the property.

Using utilities like electricity or gas without permission.

Fly-tipping.

They're bringing in fence posts and wire, Adam said.

Kaplan clears you out, I said, then he'll go after the rest of us.

Adam showed me a pair of wire cutters.

Put a fence up today, he said, and I'll cut it down tomorrow.

There were other people at the camp. Summer visitors.

Dawn and Lala, teenage runaways from a gang of men who'd raped and prostituted them. Gloster Vince, an army veteran camped in the hollow of a dead tree inside a perimeter of sharpened sticks. Conor, an ancient former navvy, who had lost the ability to speak in a way that could be understood.

Bloke called Jason. Gnomic, balding under a cap, mostly smiling though he had his quiet sad days. Lots of teeth missing so he had an underbite like a bulldog. Insides were kaput, you could tell by looking at him. Yellow. Around thirty but looked closer to my age. For some reason he called me Paul.

All right Paul?

Jason played an imaginary guitar. He was very convincing. Fingers seemed to know what they were doing. A small cardboard sign said: Guitar lessons.

Walked into the camp one day and Jason was sitting with his back to a tree, waving a stick up and down.

All right Paul? he said.

The sign offering guitar lessons was gone.

What happened to the guitar? I said.

Gave it up.

Why?

Too many groupies Paul.

What you doing now?

Conducting.

Fur hat on the ground. A sign next to it that said: Beware of the dog.

Mind how you go Paul, Jason said.

There's something I've been thinking about, I said to Adam, and told him.

Kaplan's house across the river seemed to exist in starbursts, blazing from every window in the house and from the marquee that was set up on the big lawn. There were ropes of fairy lights in the fading rhododendrons. A young woman moved among the guests with a tray of drink and food, her skin made darker by the waist-to-ankle white apron that she wore, the shining foreground.

Where the garden met the river there was a jetty or little pier. Kaplan's cruiser was alongside, gleaming. Alexandra, barefoot in a white halter-top dress, her red hair loose, half-walked half-ran along the jetty and stepped onto the boat with the tall blonde boy she was holding by the hand. I didn't know if it was the boy called Dex, but I couldn't be sure it wasn't.

A reggae tune started and was turned up, and the lawn became full of dancing kids. Through the windows of the boat, I could see Alexandra's outline dancing close with the boy.

Adam threw the eviction notice on my cold fire.

I know a place, he said. Let's go.

Now?

You got anything better to do?

I need to bring anything?

Got a torch? I need a piss.

We stood up and moved around getting ready. The boat see-sawed a little on the water. The tyre fenders creaked loudly. A light came on in John Rose's boat. Adam went into the stall and pissed like a horse and I worried my portaloo was going to overflow.

What? he said when he came out.

I found my torch and put it in my bag. Red stood up.

Dog coming with us? Adam said.

John Rose didn't have time to look after a dog. That's

what he said. Almost without realizing it Red was with me all the time. I'd made a bed for her on the floor, but more often than not she'd sneak into my narrow bunk and squeeze herself next to me. So that we shored each other up. I'd open my eyes in the morning and find myself face to face with her. Hot breath a fishy wave. If I didn't move quickly to let her out she'd lick my face and I became used to this unusual start to the day.

Looks like, I said.

She know to keep quiet?

Red's ears were up and she turned her head to look at both of us as we spoke.

Well, I said, wherever it is we're going she'll let us know if somebody else is there.

Somebody is there, Adam said.

I looked at him but all he said was: Let's go.

The party music got louder. Tales of Babylon and sufferation boomed across the illuminated lawns. Bass lines rolled over the river. Adam looked at me but said nothing and we went into the forest towards the boatyard. The treetops bent and sshhed against one another in a wind we did not feel at ground level. There were birds up there too. Dark movement, the sound of wings. The light of the new moon showed faintly on the path and the rough sides of trees. Little flashes came from the forest on either side. Unseen animals made quick scraping sounds as they moved through the dry undergrowth. Red, silent, tensed at each sound and turned her head. Stayed on the path. Adam's back was a big slab I couldn't see past.

We came out at the boatyard. The new security lights on the big fence came on.

Adam turned and headed west on a narrow path, between the trees and the moonlit water. We went deeper into the forest until the music could only just be heard.

I'd never been in this part of the island before.

Red stopped suddenly. She pricked her ears and peeled off into the forest. A girl materialized on the path in front of me. Short, dyed-blonde hair shaved at the sides, pink fluffy sweater with the sleeves pushed up to her elbows. The girl's hair and jumper were dirty but oddly luminous. She wore cut-offs, and shower shoes over socks. She held something down by her side. A screen or a blade flashing blue in the moonlight.

What are you doing here? she said.

A foreign voice, Eastern European. A tough, boy's face, with high cheekbones, thin lips, no make-up. Dirty, fugitive, but with her shit together. Seventeen at most. Hard eyes.

I live here, I said, on the other side.

You can tell me stories, she said, what looked like mosquito bites on her bare forearms, but who knows who you are.

Some kind of rune tattooed on the side of her head I could see.

Hey Nina.

Adam had doubled back.

Adam, the girl said. He's with you?

Yeah.

All right then, the girl called Nina said.

She stepped off the path and vanished, her bright hair and jumper the last of her to be visible.

Who's that? I said.

Adam looked at me, his face both light and dark.

That's Nina.

She in the camp?

That's right.

What's she doing out here?

I don't know. Not my business. Mate of Dawn's.

I was about to whistle for Red when she appeared on the path, white markings brightest in the near dark.

We came to a chain link fence. Inside I could see some kind of hangar or silo.

The fence shimmered. Adam looked at me, the pale moon haloing his head made his broken face seem golden. Adam trailed his fingers along the fence and it rattled.

At the big padlock Adam took something from his back pocket. Seconds later we were on the other side. I looked at him.

I'm in and out of here all the time, he said.

Adam reached through the fence and re-locked the padlock.

Bats fizzed jerkily all around us.

A large structure made of metal, with a curvilinear roof that corresponded to or made an answering pattern with the underside of the risen moon. A low, fast vibrating noise coming from inside.

The shape of the hangar or silo seemed fated given my

vision of the dark ovals suggested by the reflected arches of the bridge far downstream.

At the front there was a huge sliding iron door that Adam got open as easily as he had the big padlock. The vibrating noise got louder.

Light flooded the space from strips high above us.

Gene was using a belt sander on the hull of a fishing boat. The boat was up on a kind of cradle made of boards and scaffolding, and Gene was working underneath. Paint flakes and dust fell to a plastic sheet that covered the space under the boat. The boat was the classic type – wheelhouse, open deck with gunwales. The hull would contain the sleeping compartment, a tiny galley and head, with a small space for storage in the bow. No engine that I could see.

Gene turned off the sander. Looked at us. Wearing a grubby handkerchief over his mouth and nose so that all I could see were his huge eyes that had new light in them. Took a flat chisel from his pocket and worked at some stubborn paint. Threw the chisel down onto the plastic sheet and looked at us again.

Fuck's sake Adam, he said through the cloth.

Sucking and blowing out the material as he talked. Gene pulled down the handkerchief and spat, careful to aim beyond the plastic sheet. Rubbed his head free of dust and paint. Shook the rest of himself out like a dog. There was a bottle of beer by his feet and he reached down and picked it up. Wiped the top and drank from it. Every time he moved the plastic underneath his feet made sticking and pulling sounds.

You're building a boat, I said.

Nothing gets past the bloke, Gene said.

Red went over to be petted, her feet on the plastic making rapid versions of the sounds Gene made.

In the corner I could see a sleeping bag. Some of Gene's clothes.

Get out of there Red, I said.

I walked around the space with Red following. The floor was gritty underfoot.

Power points. Overhead strip lighting. A big plywood tool board mounted on the wall by the work tables. I ran my hands across work surfaces, opening drawers.

It's perfect, I said.

For what? Gene said.

Tell him what you told me, Adam said.

How big are you talking? Gene said when I'd finished.

You want to be able to see them from the river, I said. How high's the roof here?

High enough, said Adam, looking up.

Gene looked at me moving around. Looked at Adam.

Dreamland, he said. The pair of you.

Slowly passed my hand over the hull of Gene's boat.

Must have taken a while.

Me and Michael started her, he said. Brought her up the river when she wasn't much more than a wreck. Do her up, sell her, that was the plan.

Then when we lost him, I'd work on her for Perseis. You

146

heard her. Been together since we was seventeen, he said. Still thought I could have killed Mike.

You all right? I said.

Gene looked at me the way he had the first time we'd met. After the cops had let him go for the umpteenth time. Like he had no use for me and never would. A stranger passing through his world.

Course I'm not all right, Gene said. What do you think? Fucking cursed. Fucking start again. Couldn't go before. Look like I was running away.

Any news from the divers?

You seen any divers? he said. Cos I fucking haven't.

I had seen police launches on the river, but no divers.

I looked up at the boat.

Need an engine, I said.

Working on it.

Gene turned and ducked back under the poles and looked up at his boat.

Shouldn't be using a belt sander, he said. Makes the hull too flat, but you gotta use the tools you have.

Gene blew on the hull, raising a cloud of dust. Rubbed the spot with his sweatshirted elbow. Pulled his handkerchief back up over and his mouth and nose.

Looked down at me, the cloth covering his face. Raised the belt sander in a salute and turned to his work. The raw whine of the sander started up as we left the hangar.

Cost money, Adam said as we walked back.

What does? I said.

We should talk to John, he said.

Adam was right. The supplies I needed would cost. More than I had certainly. But the old man didn't have any money to spare, far as I knew.

Your goldfinches, Adam said.

What about them?

You think they just happen to come back where they do, every year?

Didn't know the first thing about goldfinches or where they came from.

John buys this special seed, Adam said. Niger seed. The goldfinches love it. Been putting it down for years. That's why they come back to that tree, right by John's boat.

Does Gene know that Anthony Waters is Brady Millar?

Who's Brady Millar when he's at home? Adam said.

I told him.

Are you sure?

You think I should tell Gene?

Does it make any difference? Adam said.

Brady Millar was a fighter, I said.

Right, Adam said. I see what you're saying.

You think I should talk to him?

I'm gonna think about it, the giant youth said.

We were nearly home when the explosions started. Red began trembling and barking. Adam scooped her up and cradled her, the dog wild-eyed and panting heavily at each clattering blast. Fireworks bloomed like bursting shells in the sky above the moorings.

Don't worry sweetheart, I said to the dog in the giant's arms, it's just noise.

I could make out Alex Kaplan on his cultured lawn, bathed in gunpowder smoke. The big rockets flew upwards, burning and falling over the river and close to the boats.

Kaplan white-shirted, bent over the rockets with a lighted taper in his hand.

Close as I was to the canvas, John Rose's wool hat was a giant black field, shining where it was still wet. Have to move down the ladder to see his face. Get off the ladder entirely and move over to where Adam and Gene, wearing masks, were shaking paint cans and spraying, if I wanted to get an idea of how the whole thing was working out. Better to trust the small painting I'd made of the old man on *Vesna*. Put a numbered grid over this picture, and before sizing the big canvas I'd replicated the grid to scale. Stuck and re-stuck the little picture where I could always see it. To the canvas. The side of the ladder. Be working blind otherwise. I applied the black paint thickly and twisted the brush into the canvas to replicate the curl of the wool.

We'd cut the wood for the giant stretchers, and worked the great sheets of canvas over the finished frames. Every-thing had to be done properly, but to this new scale. Paid particular attention to the detail of the corner folds, which on frames this size involved a lot of material. Everything was a two- or three-person job.

The massive, awkward to handle canvasses were stacked up against the hangar's wall.

Took huge amounts of rabbit skin glue to size the can-vasses, but it was the fumes from the spray paint that made me risk working with the big doors open.

Come on Dan, I said. Fresh air time.

Oh man, the boy said.

Now, son.

Danny wore a bandana over his nose and mouth like the men. All day Goldie and the other kids had been running in and out to see him, bringing with them little artworks they had made: colourings, plasticine flowers, dogs and boats made from shiny foil, carved polystyrene horses with pink felt-tip manes.

Put them in the trees, I said.

Where? Goldie said.

By Michael's stones, Danny said.

Working from a double-platformed trestle tower, the boy was helping Adam and Gene paint a big mural of the island on hardwood panels.

Came slowly down the ladder. Lowered his bandana and looked at me from the platform.

Oh man, he said again. What about Adam? And Gene?

Gene coughed into his bandana, his face behind the material making broken shapes.

Go on son, he said once he'd finished.

The first thing I'd heard Gene say all day.

Danny sighed and held up his arms.

Lift me, the boy said.

Taking an arm each Adam and Gene lifted him over the side of the trestle tower and then lowered him until his boots were level with my face.

Now, I said, and caught the boy when the men dropped him. A heavy weight.

Red was waiting in the sun. She wouldn't come into the painting room, but stayed outside, patrolling the fence line, or sunning herself in the yard that was overgrown with dandelions and the long spikes of flowering hollyhocks tall as the boy. The vertical line disclosed.

Eyes shut, Danny walked on wobbly legs, his hands to his head.

Ooohhhh, he said.

Danny, I said. Danny! You all right?

The boy opened his eyes.

Ha! Fooled you, he said, and ran away with the dog.

I scratched at the dried paint on my arms and under my fingernails, smoked a roll-up and watched Danny and Red chase after wobbling butterflies and fat bees in the shimmering sunshine. Red let the boy hold her and push his face into her warm fur. In the middle of the game the boy suddenly became serious and rushed back to the hangar, pulling the bandana back up over his face. A boy with a cause. Red chased him to the doorway but no further. She came to me, walking slowly and looking very serious and responsible. Always the sound of water. In the direction of the river the low light between the dark trees was a radiant silver. I gave the dog a piece of cold sausage from my pocket. She smacked her jaws.

Let me know if you hear anybody coming, I said.

Red lay down next to the water bowl with her head between her front paws, looking towards the shining treeline.

Started to go inside and then came back out and gave

Red another piece of sausage. Leaned down and kissed her on the nose.

You're a good girl, I said. Yes you are.

Everybody gave what they could or what they wanted to, John had said when he gave me the cash.

There won't be any more.

Gene and I had brought the materials upstream by small tender on an afternoon so clear the arched bridge of Portland stone behind us was reflected in the sky.

The wind made briefly expanding patterns on the surface of the river. Unnameable shapes that quickly disappeared to be replaced by others. The boat low in the water, laden with art materials: canvas, timber for stretchers, plywood, tubs of size, brushes and paints – acrylics and canisters of spray paint – fixative, cable ties, boxes of nails, all of it wrapped under tarpaulin like contraband. Gene tied up at the boatyard jetty and we made several trips to the hangar to unload the stuff.

I held on to the ladder tight with one hand, pressing my knees into it, with my free hand dipping the big decorator brush into the tray of paint balanced on the rung – a mix of red, yellow and brown to make the sandstone colour of his skin – and applied paint to John's huge painted likeness. It was like painting the side of a mountain.

There's a tradition of English painting in which the portrait of the subject is framed or surrounded by a series of smaller pictures showing scenes from the subject's life.

Victories and defeats. Births and deaths. I'd seen this kind of work in country shows and fairs, the sides of wooden caravans, the painted backdrop of the boxing booth, and in fact on championship belts splashed with the blood of both winner and loser. I'd seen it on painted flatware and scrimshawed ivory, on the banners of trade unions raised high above the stones and fire of demonstration.

I was painting John Rose and the others with this in mind. Deciding on scenes by the stories they had told me. Around the big portrait the old man's medallions included a picture of him on the deck of a burning merchant ship, sharks in the water, another dancing with Vesna at the Caribbean club after the war. Holding Nancy his infant daughter. Standing alone and ramrod straight by the painted barge.

Vesna would have liked to have somebody make her picture, John said when I went to make the study for the big painting.

I don't mean she was vain, he said. Just it would have tickled her. Sorry if I moved.

I was very careful with the small preparatory paintings or studies, protecting them with scavenged bubble wrap and placing them in cardboard pockets I'd made when I was not using them. In a notebook I dated all the studies and my progress on each big canvas.

Walking with Red through the forest so late at night it was almost morning, my head would be full of energy and my body dead tired. I'd fall back into my bunk without washing the paint from my hands and face so that in drying the paint made my skin tighten.

Not going to stop. I'd place paintings on every surface I could find, hang them in the trees, paint directly onto the trees, float pictures on rafts down the river, make the rafts themselves works of art. Not just paintings but art works of all kinds. More nature sculptures, like Michael's cairn, and sculptures made from materials found and scavenged from the island.

The painted island would become known all over the world, and because of this it would be protected. The art made permanent. The paintings would not be for sale.

Evelyn Crow would not be able to make the art disappear. Nor anybody like him.

Then I would hear the goldfinches singing and Red would be awake and looking at me, mouth slightly open. A kind of still, silent panting. Keeping vigil or waiting to be fed.

The spray paint fumes were really getting to me.

I gave John Rose young eyes. Restored the crumbling irises to strong rings. Added silver to faded grey. I guessed John had contributed the lion's share of the money I was to spend on supplies. The old man wouldn't say, of course. John would want me to believe that the art project was well supported.

I was so short of money I was fanatical in making sure I got receipts for all of the materials so that I could account for everything. If John was surprised to see each penny justified he didn't show it.

Don't make this about Adam and the camp, John had said. People paid their money for you to represent them in this fight, not a bunch of damn squatters.

When did you leave the navy?

John had covered the floor of his boat with a tarpaulin sheet.

I had to pack in the merchant ships, John said, once I was married and the baby came. Vesna would not stand for me gallivanting around from port to port.

The old man smiled to himself. Ran a finger along the long-gone moustache. We were sharp for shore leave, he said, nodding at the photo of the two young men with their arms around each other's shoulders. Me and Billy there. Had a man in Hong Kong make us three suits at a time. I must say we cut a dash.

Why'd you go to sea in the first place? I said.

What's that? Take that blessed thing out of your mouth.

The paintbrush, he meant.

What made you go to sea?

Ever since I was a little chap I wanted to travel the world. Who knows the world better than the British Merchant Navy? Java. Rangoon. The Indian Ocean and the Pacific. The China seas. I have travelled up the Nile, he said. Walked in the streets of Constantinople and Timbuktu. Seen flying fish at first light. Wept at the Gate of No Return.

Must have been tough, I said. Leaving all that. Missed the sea.

Stay outside, he called to Red, who was peering in at us

from the open cabin door, her face and ears a configuration of triangles.

I loved Vesna, John had said. How much longer are you going to be?

Come and look Terry, Danny called out from the other side of the hangar.

Carrying the paint tray I came slowly down, the wood handle of the paintbrush between my teeth. Descending past John's giant face. Rinsed out my brush with cold water and left it on the big draining board of the Belfast sink. Crossed the big space passing the finished and unfinished pictures that were wrapped and stacked against the wall. Like being on site and in the studio at the same time.

I looked back at John's portrait.

What do you think? Danny said.

The mural was being painted on three large plywood boards.

Danny had drawn the original picture, crayoning and felt-tipping in the bright colours on a piece of card. I'd replicated Danny's picture on the boards, just the line work, using the grid system again, writing in the names of the colours to be added.

Three of the sections were finished, strong and clear like new graffiti seen from a train window. The teardrop-shaped island was painted a vibrant green, the river blue, with the recognizable figures of John, Stella and Danny, Gene, Perseis and others waving and smiling from bright decorated barges. Adam and dogs in the camp. A porpoise arching through the water. The dogs Red and Choo-Choo on the foreshore. Even the rose-pink bridge.

The boards, though big, were individually portable, and the whole mural could be assembled or disassembled. Gene made eyelets in the corners of each board so that we could put cable ties through and lash them.

Gene and Adam put down their spray cans. Both pulled down their bandanas. Like Danny their faces were half clean and half sprayed with multi-coloured paint.

Danny had begged to be allowed to use the spray paints.

Can you help him? I'd asked Adam.

I'll help the kid, Gene said.

I was amazed to see Gene's strong outlines, his confident use of colour.

Put up enough tags in my time, he said when I asked him.

I didn't know that, I said.

You never asked, he said, rattling a can.

You tell him about Millar? I'd asked Adam.

She's better off with him, Adam said.

Gene tell you that? I'd said.

Adam had nodded.

You think Gene will go after him?

Gene won't hurt Perseis, Adam had said. But his heart's broken, so who knows?

In the painting a dark-haired Michael sailed a dinghy on the river. Gene passed his fingers over the figures of Perseis and Michael without touching them.

Danny looked at Gene, his decorated face expression-less, and nodded.

How long before it's finished? I said.

We stood in front of the vast panels of bright colour.

Tomorrow, next day, latest, Adam said.

Gene brought the little flat-bottomed Zodiac around, tying off at a buoy made from an old green jerry can and a weighted line. The tender moving gently on the riffling current, too small-looking for the job. Gene waded ashore.

Pointed the camera at him without turning it on.

Gene a dark figure all in black, heavy boots. Adam a silent giant by his side.

Waiting for the full moon to rise.

For the river to become a lighted highway. Bright enough to see.

Sack full of ropes, bungee cords and thick black cable ties. Video camera. No lights. We wore dark clothes and while we were waiting, Gene and I muddied our faces.

My secret wish was for swans flying across the swollen moon as we ferried the paintings downriver. For the paintings to be suddenly everywhere in the morning.

You still got that video camera? I'd asked John.

What camera?

The old man was using a Stanley knife to cut the plastic ties on a box of protest leaflets.

Gone to beg for some of his life-giving brew. Remembered the home movies he'd shown at Michael's celebration.

Tired and so stiff I could hardly stand, but my head fizzed with ideas, and I hadn't slept in days.

Don't come in, John had said, passing me a brimming cup.

Red licked at the wet paint on my leg.

Knock it off, Red, I said.

The camera you used to make all your films, I'd said through the narrow opening. And I'll need to borrow the Zodiac.

I could even show John's films with the new footage I was planning to shoot. Make it all the same film.

The old man disappeared inside with the leaflets. Was gone long enough for the coffee to have cooled if I hadn't gulped it down at once.

These are mine, John said, handing me a bag with the heavy camera and its housing inside.

The knife blade he'd left on the little sill was free of rust and gleaming.

The Zodiac key was on a stretchable lanyard with a carabiner at the other end, and I attached the clip to my belt loop and stuffed the key and lanyard in my pocket.

Interval of John coughing and me pretending not to notice. Blood on his cheek.

Are you listening? John had said.

There's one other thing, I'd said.

In the hangar I'd wrapped the mural panels and three of the massive paintings in sacking and tarpaulin, and tied them with rope. Painted numbers on them so I'd know which was which. The huge pictures were stacked up against a couple of ash trees. Another stack of paintings were wrapped up in the hangar. For the weir and the boatyard fence.

Can you take charge of these other paintings? I'd asked the old man. They need to go up on the weir. Danny will help you.

You want me with the boy? was all the old man said.

Here came the moon.

Filmed Adam and Gene as they lifted the first panel of the mural and carried it to the Zodiac, wading through shin-high water. Through the lens they were dark figures about some obscure business. Poachers, drug smugglers. Partisans.

The men laid the picture flat so that it was balanced across the boat's inflatable sides. Adam held the panel in place while Gene, using three long bungee cords linked together and hooked to the handholds of the boat, worked quickly to lash the painting down.

The panel and the boat moved around as Gene was working to secure it, and Adam had to fight to hold everything in place. I held my breath. Could hear Gene swearing. The splashing the men made as they moved heavily around. When they came out of the water they were both soaked to the waist, and Gene was breathing hard.

Adam looked at Gene.

Hands on knees.

Fuck, he said, and spat on the ground.

Give me the camera, he said at last.

What? I said.

You think we're going to hump all these onto the boat while you sit on your arse watching?

I'm working.

Looking at him through the lens.

Give me the camera, he said.

I turned the camera to the lighted houseboats. Nobody was moving around, but I knew we were being watched.

I turned the camera back on Gene.

Gene, I said.

I swear, said Gene, making a fist and covering the camera lens with his other hand, if you say one word about art I'll stick one on you.

Have you lost your minds? said a voice from the trees.

Stella. Red alongside.

Gene, she said, pull up to the shore and then load up.

She's right, I said. Where have you been?

With Danny and John Rose, Stella said. What have you got on your faces?

Adam pulled the boat onto the foreshore, mud sucking at his boots.

Gene raised the outboard engine so that the screw was pulled up above the waterline.

Adam and Gene loaded the two remaining mural panels, unhooking two bungee cords to add another so that the cords would reach around the bigger pile.

Started carrying one of the giant portraits to the boat.

We'll make two trips, Stella said.

Adam and Gene put the painting down.

I'll stay, I said.

I filmed Adam and Gene pushing the boat into the river. Gene jumped in while Adam held her steady. Gene sat in the transom to the left of the outboard , the stacked paintings in front of him, his head level with the highest.

The mural boards were much wider than the boat, and rested on and stuck out over the inflated tubing. Stella climbed in on the other side to Gene. She lowered the engine so that the screw was in the water. Moved to the bow and turned the key.

All right Adam, she called, above the sound of the engine.

Adam, soaking, hauled himself into the bow.

They set off.

Stella steered into the path made by the reflected moon.

The boat was too low in the water, and went very slowly. I filmed them until they were out of sight, the dancing skirt of white water made by the boat the last thing I saw. I looked hard downstream. Even with the moon the bulk of the bridge was a dark mass spanning the river. The deep arches seemed filled-in and made solid by the dark. Now and then a vehicle crossed over, the car or van itself lighted, so that even from that distance I could make out the shape or shapes of its occupants before it passed into the darkness that was the world beyond my sight.

I stopped filming when I could no longer hear the boat.

First the sound of the engine was gone, then the echo of the sound came and went. I rolled a cigarette.

Something broke the surface of the water upstream. Bird call. A light on a boat switched on and off. Fenders creaked. Whoosh of water as a night bird landed. Boots on the weir. Moving slowly. Carrying something heavy.

Red flumped down by my side and together we dreamed.

Engine clatter opened my eyes. The boat slowly appeared out of the dark. Chugging along. Gene in the bow, higher in the water now. Stella turned off the engine and coasted in. Gene threw me the rope and I caught it.

The wooden floor of the boat was littered with bungee cords and smeared with muddy water. We loaded up again and set off.

Red ran into the water and started swimming after the Zodiac.

Go back Red! I said, go back!

Go back Red! Go back! said Stella.

Red! Red!

Before we reached deep water the dog made a wide half circle turn and swam back to the shore. When she came out of the water I could hear her shaking herself. Barked three times from the river's edge.

There were low, fast-moving breakers out in the channel, white horses and all, and the flat-bottomed tender hit and passed over them hard like they were made of concrete. Black water chopped and splashed into the boat.

Filmed everything one-handed, the other pushing down on the covered pictures. Holding myself in place by jamming my feet against the steering column. Gene was holding on hard to the pictures, his fingers candle-white.

Stella's fair hair blown all around by the wind we made in our passing. Gave me the thumbs up.

From so low down in the water the bridge was sheer and huge. The arches were great dark caves. I leaned back in the boat and filmed it that way.

Under the bridge Stella cut the engine. A single whistle came from the riverbank. Gene stood in the bow and threw the rope, which looped palely in the darkness. The rope tightened, and we were being hauled in.

Ashore, the paintings unloaded, Adam said, Mural's done.

Threw the heaped pile of tarpaulin and sacking into the boat.

Adam and Gene clambered up the shallow riverbank carrying a painting. I filmed them, then gave Gene the camera while Stella and I took the next.

We lifted the painting over the side. I had to hold the whole by holding half. Hand on the edge of the canvas, other under the corner fold where there was a natural handgrip. The rest of the picture was a dead weight. Had to almost will it in place. Below me in the darkness, Stella began lashing the painting to the outside of the bridge.

Engine to my right. Lights showed on the camber of the bridge. Towards the sky like searchlights. The car slowly crested the rise and the lights became horizontal, pointed straight at us.

Advanced. The wheels turned slowly against the surface of the bridge, making plump, gritty contact.

Stella switched to the other side. Half of the painting tied down. Easier, not pulling away but still heavy.

Rough edges of the paint-heaped canvas under my fingers.

My back to the car. An impression of light and move-ment. Turned my head far as I could. The car was just a dark box shape behind the lights it carried. Single driver. Alone. Turned my head the other way. Couldn't see Gene or Adam.

The car lights messed with my vision. Far below me the river was full of fast-moving silver snakes.

Stella?

Couldn't see what she was doing.

Company, I said.

Just a sec, she said.

Something in her mouth. Cable tie.

The car was not going past. Going slower.

Stella.

Hang on!

The car crept towards me.

OK, Stella said.

I let go. The painting held.

Let out the breath I'd been holding.

Stella stood up.

Put her arms around me. Heart beating fast. I could feel the heat of her body right through me.

Almost in slow motion the car came alongside.

Dark clothes. Ducked his head to look at us across the empty passenger seat. Nothing to see. Man and a woman on the bridge. Moon on the water. No sign of anything else. Kept on looking. Straightened up. Foot on the accelerator. Just a fraction. Carried on past.

Terry, Stella said, look.

Dull gold letters on the side. *Island Security*. Some kind of badge. Private cop.

Turned our heads to watch him pass. Stella's warm breath against my cheek. Hands on my shoulders. The driver looked at me and Stella, and back at me again. The car went past, then turned its nose left. Pulled in. Stopped. Door opened. Engine still running. Lights on. Driver got out.

Big fat bloke. No other way to say it. With him came the rank scent of a car deodorizer. Several little pine trees were still swinging on the rear view mirror.

My age, older even. Could have been wearing a uniform, or his own clothes. All black. Torchlight. Pointed at us.

Evening folks, he said. Running a film in his head. Sheriff.

Plastic or tin badge pinned to his shirt. Some kind of radio or walkie-talkie on his belt. Looked at me. Hard and slow. Back to Stella. Smiled. Could hear him thinking.

You new? he said.

What? Stella said.

I haven't seen you before, the fat man said.

Public bridge, I said.

Stella kicked me.

What's that? he said.

Public bridge. Don't have to answer questions.

Put his hands on his belt. Fat and clean. Near the radio if that's what it was. Looked at me. Looked at Stella.

You from the island? he said.

What's it to you? Stella said.

My father was a lighterman, the guard said. Upriver. You wouldn't know what that is.

I did, but I didn't say so. Lightermen unloaded goods from barge to the quay, quay to barge. Flat-bottomed boat. No sail no motor. Nothing but oar power and secret knowledge of the water. Generations. River knowledge handed down.

Weren't none left when I come of age, the fat man said. No use for them. Between the docks and the containers.

Sighed deeply.

You girls have been told about working on the bridge, he said.

What the fuck? Stella said.

My old man told me, the river's there for what you can get out of it. What I mean is, he said, could you do me like you just did him?

Stella had been crouched down in the dark. Close to my waist. I was too old to be her boyfriend.

Step to him. Bust him up. Get the fat fuck out of here.

What's your name? Stella said.

The fat man stopped chewing.

What? he said.

I work for Alexandra Kaplan, Stella said. Sure she'd like to know we have a troll living under this bridge.

Look, the guard said, hands up.

No, Stella said. I want your name.

A blur materialized. Red. Half sized because she was soaked through. Stood in front of us and spread her feet. Firm stance. She bared her teeth at the fat guard.

Take his arm off at the shoulder, Red, I said.

Couldn't get out of there fast enough. Burning rubber. Let him go. Pretended to forget we hadn't got his name.

You all right? I said.

Stella, arms folded across herself, nodded.

You think he was for real? she said.

Red shook herself back to three-quarter size.

Knew a bloke who wore a sailor's hat with captain written on the front in black marker, I said. Walked about giving orders: full steam ahead, fire the torpedoes. Didn't make him a captain.

We travelled against the current. Cold water sprayed against my face. Gene sat on the transom. Looking straight ahead. Sometimes glancing at Stella. Red sat next to Gene and stared into his face, her fur curling up in the wind we made. There was a swan that flew across the moon after all that.

You think we're going to change the world with a few pictures? Stella said. Fair hair whipping round as her words were carried downriver.

Don't know about that, I said, but have you asked yourself why a big corporation like Kaplan International would have just one security guard looking after the whole island?

Because they're not taking us seriously, Stella said.

John Rose found me and Red before first light the next morning. Wrapped in blankets. Backs against the wheelhouse, looking downstream.

Surface mist curled away, making holes you could see the water through. The bridge and my paintings would soon be revealed. If the paintings had survived the night. We'd got the go-ahead from the council, but even so the reaction of Alex Kaplan was an unknown. Been trying to work out the odds. Undiscovered or discovered. If discovered, further odds as to whether the pictures would be left up or taken down. Safe keeping or destroyed.

Stella had said: I pitched the paintings as a community arts project – which is true – and it wasn't campaigning for anything – also true. All they wanted to know was if this was part of the Save the Island group. Clearly, they were rattled by the possibility. But they heard me out, and it was fine. The only condition was that if the council request removal then we take them down.

The council, I'd said, not Kaplan?

That's right.

Single birds sang speculative phrases. Almost unnoticed the voices were joined, the songs connected. More birdsong as it became lighter, until no bird sang alone. Hooting calls sounded across the river. Echoing dog bark. The river randomly breaking open to rising fish. Somewhere a spring-hinged screen door banged shut.

You sleep?

John Rose handed me the coffee I'd been drooling over since he'd started to make it half an hour before. The mug thick, cracked. Not usual. Looked into his face against the vault of sky.

John looked tired and his colour was bad. Dry. Ashy. Hand a bit shaky.

I hadn't slept. Close my eyes and the paintings were there and not there. Changed everything and changed nothing. Given a parade and got myself locked up. An endless loop.

No, I said. You?

At my age you need all the time awake you can get, John said.

How old are you?

Never asked him before. Never dared.

John scratched the dog's ears. Red leaned into his hands.

I won't see eighty-six again, he said, or eighty-seven either.

Speaking seemed to take effort. Words forced across a great plain of time.

The old man's glasses were smeared. Dirty long johns under his reefer coat. Straight arm corded with thick veins. Muscles fighting softness. Losing.

You have any trouble at the weir? I said.

I'd wanted everything done at once. Should have waited.

Done it myself, today. My body was sore all over from hoisting the paintings around. Had to think John would be hurting twice as much. More.

They're up, aren't they? he said.

Gone straight to the weir after we'd got back from the bridge.

Danny keeping watch.

More islander portraits were secured to the side of the weir, above the roaring fall of water. Tuppy Lawrence. Gene and Perseis. Adam, surrounded by dogs, foliate-headed and costumed in ferns and berry sprigs.

Danny, his face pale with tiredness, was sitting with his hands and arms wrapping his knees, his back against the iron structure. The boy opened his eyes and jumped up when he heard me.

Go home son, I'd said. Get some sleep.

The line of willows on the far riverbank became visible as the sun rose. Slowly then quickly. Above the willows the almost purple lawns. A kitchen light was turned off in a low white house, door opening. A composition of coloured bands: white house, the steeply inclined purple lawn, velvet willows and the paling river. A large dog, a setter by its fringed outline, streaked from the open door down the centre of the lawn in a fast chestnut line. At the river's edge the dog stood looking out, barking, setting off reverberations that seemed to make the boats buck in slow motion on the water. Red answered happily and I put my arm round her.

Star-crossed lovers, I said, my hand moving in her cool fur.

Red licked my face.

Sitting upright, her jaws slightly parted, giving full attention to sounds only she could hear. Eyes dancing.

Monty!

The calling voice of the dog's owner came echoing across the river.

John laughed very quietly.

There were no spires or crosses in my wide-angled view, but from somewhere in the distance came the sound of Sunday church bells.

John lifted his head a fraction.

The lightness in the sky spread. Mist chased away by the warming air. The river like tin. The bridge became the softest of coral pinks. Sun rays flaring through the arches.

Red shook off her blanket and stood up and I did the same.

The pictures were still there.

The faces of John Rose, Michael, Stella and Danny showed high on the bridge and in brilliant angled reflection on the water.

Artwork of the floating people. Twenty feet high. Bigger than kings.

John Rose leaned out in his canvas chair. Wiped his glasses.

Heavens, the old man said.

Clouds swept upstream, and the pictures and the bridge were lost to clear view.

The old man put his hand on my shoulder and pushed himself up. Stood for a bit.

You leave any juice in the tank? he said finally.

Course.

We'd cleaned the Zodiac of mud before putting her back alongside John's barge. Tuppy had donated a can of diesel.

Let's take a closer look.

Smiling.

Followed John across to his boat, my boots on the deck making a sound like somebody chopping wood in the distance. Got in the Zodiac, the tender in shadow, wide rubber sides still wet with dew. Sat down on the transom and looked around at the new day. Red curled at my feet, out of the way. A river dog, a good sailor. John brought us slowly out to open water. The sun felt good.

Two minutes later I wished I'd worn warmer clothes. The wind kicked up waves and spray and pushed the clouds along. Sun breaking through but not for long. Red snapped at the river froth that flew into the boat.

John kept us out of the path of bigger waves I never saw coming. The movement of a finger, the palm of his hand. Holding the boat to the position he wanted. Putting just enough on it so that we were not pushed back by the current I could feel moving beneath the thin wooden flooring. The water thumped against the inflated and pressurized sides.

Tug boat on our stern, *Reclaim*, the bow gunwales painted orange. Pulling a barge loaded with containers all different shades of yellow: sand, lion, daffodil, sunshine. The pilot was looking up from the river to the paintings on the bridge. Looked across and did a double take as he recognized John. Sounded his horn and gave us the thumbs up.

Red jumped up and span around, barking.

The tug pilot was listening to the radio. I could see the antenna on the wheelhouse. An old song, 'Pretty Flamingo', that Nan used to sing in the kitchen on Sunday mornings when I was a kid . . . *and paradise is where I'll be*. Heard John, shading his eyes as he looked at the paintings, humming as the song was taken away on the wind. Da dada daa.

Clouds separated once more. John kept the boat parallel, passing along and looking up at the three paintings, then turning the little inflatable boat and coming by again. Hands always moving on the wheel he never looked at.

People looking from the towpaths either side of the river. Dog walkers, an early morning runner in all the gear. The runner slowed to a stop, jogging on the spot as he looked up at the paintings.

From the low tender John gazed up at the steep and massive portraits, looking at himself, studying the painted scenes from his life. Birth and love and war. All his untold, unnoticed history was up on the bridge. Now you had to see him. Everybody who fought the wars and built the homes and farmed the land and fished the seas and raised the kids was up there.

Wind and spray kicked up off the river and blew against us and John wiped his face and I did too. Then the old man turned and smiled and that was enough for me.

Light burst from Michael's picture. Michael underwater. Arms stretched wide. White face. Above the tall, up-reaching kelp beds, through columns of cathedral sur-face light. Black hair streaming behind him. Painting washed in varieties of river green. Almost hidden in the kelp forest I'd placed a painted cairn of pale smooth stones.

Found river treasure placed and held under a thick film of gel mixed with silver glitter Danny had donated, so that Michael's was the heaviest and the brightest picture.

A boy born into a world of painted barges. The living colour in the forest. The river. Michael might be lost for-ever, but he was held in the embrace of his place and people.

Goodness, John said.

The old man coughed and spat something over the side, then put two fingers back on the wheel and made a small correction to our position in the water.

Some people won't like it, John said. Think you're get-ting something for it.

You think it's all right to paint the boy underwater? he said.

I didn't answer.

You're cold, the old man said, let's go back.

John set off without swinging the boat round, so that we were headed under the bridge. Went into the shadow of the bridge before correcting his course and heading back to the island. Ten, fifteen minutes as the crow flies, but we'd been out on the water for over an hour.

Standing in his large garden across the river, Monty's owner, wearing a shirt and tie under a jumper, was looking at the bridge through binoculars and talking on the phone at the same time. The vertical purple field of morning was now an emerald lawn mown in straight lines. A sprinkler made rainbow circles in the air.

Michael would love it, John said, with his back to me. Get a big kick out of it.

What about you John? You get a kick out of it?

The old man turned to look at me. Said something I couldn't hear.

What?

Look after the blessed dog, he said.

The old man seemed to go out of focus and become blurred and then come back. A look of wonder on his face. Then he went out of focus again and stayed that way.

John put his hand to his heart and fell down, the side of his head hitting the wheel hard as he dropped with a thump like a door banging shut.

Red barked.

The Zodiac span wildly off course.

I scrambled forward on hands and knees. Reached over John's body. Grabbed the wheel. Pointed the bow towards the island. Let go of the wheel. Lifted John and sat him up but when I let go he fell over on his side, his head bumping on the wet wooden deck.

John!

Not breathing.

Red barking all the time.

The boat veered away again and I straightened her once more.

Kaplan's dock was up ahead. Made a beeline and began shouting and waving. The red-haired girl came running across the lawn.

She pulled her phone from her shorts pocket.

Wrenching the wheel round I cut the engine and we came in portside on, too fast, bashing hard into the dock, bouncing off, water in the boat sloshing over John. Red barking desperately, feet spread wide for balance. The boat spinning. Smash turned the key. Got power, straightened for the dock. Cut the engine. Still too fast, but the girl jumped, red hair streaming upwards so that she seemed to be jumping from her own fire. Landed with a thump and nearly lost her balance but she stayed in the boat. Scrambled for the rope. Glanced at John fallen into the well of the boat but said nothing. I fired the engine and lined up the Zodiac with the dock and cut the engine again and came in scraping rubber against wood. Alexandra jumped onto the dock holding the rope and tied us off at the bow. The stern was swinging out towards the river.

Another rope! the girl shouted.

Found a rope in the well of the boat and tied one end off at the transom and threw the other end up to her. Alexandra pulled on the rope until we were tight alongside. Feet planted, leaning back. Held on until I got John out.

The girl led the way to the house.

I carried John, Red at my heels.

Into a large, sunlit room. Dark hardwood floor. Vases of white lilies and stargazers. A side table of bottled spirits.

Glass decanter pulsing with light. Paintings on the wall that I didn't see.

I know CPR, the girl said, tucking a length of red hair behind her ear.

It's too late, I said.

Lay John down on the settee. Arranged him so that he looked as neat as possible. Pulled off his wet hat and stuffed it in my pocket.

John was soaked through. River water ran from his sodden clothes and body and onto the hardwood floor.

Can you get some towels? I said.

The girl was staring at the water running from John's body as though it were a process, a part of his dying, that would end with the body melted into air.

Some towels? I said.

It doesn't matter about the floor, she said, still staring.

For him, I said. I don't want him to get cold.

Alexandra jumped up. Wide-eyed, all arms and legs.

Course, she said. How stupid.

Get away from there Red, I said.

The paramedics came when the girl was out of the room. Heard the door, and Alexandra talking to them, and then after a minute she brought them in. A squat, bow-legged man with a pushed-in South American face, hard and soft at the same time, and a large woman with electric-blue hair extensions to her waist. Both medics were dressed in green blouse jackets and green cargo trousers. The man wore trainers, the woman thick soled boots. Surgical gloves a lighter shade of blue than the woman's hair.

I answered their questions. John Rose, he just fell down. Out on the river. Maybe a heart attack? Lot on his mind. Not sure, around ninety. Terry Godden, the island.

And what was Mr Rose to you? the blue-haired woman said.

What was he?

Who was he?

John was my neighbour, I said.

Alexandra Kaplan was looking at John over the pile of thick white towels she was holding.

And is this his dog?

Red looked hopefully at the woman when she spoke, and then at me, as if between us the noises we were making might make John appear. She recognized his name like she knew her own, and stood when she heard it. Mouth open, almost smiling, Her tail began and stopped a sideways movement, very slow, as though her body was learning a truth her mind already knew.

I put my hand on her silky ear.

Red's my dog, I said.

She licked my hand.

Buen perro, the South American man said.

Did Mr Rose have any relatives that you know of, Mr Godden?

A daughter, Nancy. I don't know where she lives. John was a widower.

The South American man was looking through a tiny address book he had taken from John's pocket. I'd never seen it before. Showed the woman a page. She nodded.

The man closed the book. Put it in the pocket of his blouse jacket.

Thank you Mr Godden, the woman said. We'll look after your friend from here.

The hammered-in seams and lines on the old man's face were set in an expression of stillness. No more wonder. All the other concentrated emotions of his life had sunk back down into him, like the raised strata, the deep long-buried stuff, returning to the riverbed when the storm has passed.

Then he was gone.

Not a relative. Couldn't go with him.

Alexandra handed me a soft towel.

You're wet, she said. And you look cold.

Thank you.

John's wet body had left a dark imprint on the settee, as though he had been suddenly dematerialized by some great force.

There were tiny islands of water forming on the hard-wood floor.

Gone but his going filled the room, pushing at the places where the walls and ceiling met, my sense of him suddenly uncontained, in danger of being blown away and lost through the open window. John's island smell was fighting a losing battle against the perfume of the pale, expensive lilies.

Red was pacing, looking for John.

Come here Red, I said.

Her tense body warmed my hands.

Alexandra went to the window. Looked out, sunlight blazing in her hair. I didn't know if she could see the river from there.

What did they ask you? I said.

What? Alexandra said.

The paramedics, I said, I heard you talking.

They wanted to know if I knew you, the girl said. Had you threatened me. They asked if I wanted to call the police.

Smoothing my beard I saw my black fingernails. Muddy bootprints all over the floor.

They wanted to know if I thought he was really hurt, Alexandra said.

The big house. The girl alone. Two desperate men lie to get inside.

I told them I knew that man, she said. John Rose. He was Michael's friend.

The dog raised her head when she heard John's name, then just as quickly put it back down. Remembered. The man's name no longer brings the man.

Then you know John Rose was one of the people your father's trying to evict, I said.

My body was not solid at the edges, but fuzzy. Tired.

I started shaking. Red looked at me, the whites of her eyes showing.

There was the very real idea that Evelyn Crow would pay me a lot of money for the paintings.

The girl put her hand on my arm.

You're still wet through, she said. You must be freezing.

Would you like a drink? Dad's always raving about the good whisky he keeps.

I shook myself. Rubbed my face.

I'd love a cup of tea, I said.

My dad says murder, she said. Murder a cup of tea, murder a drink. Murder that bugger. Milk and sugar?

Honey, I said.

Red followed the girl out of the room. I must have fallen asleep because the girl woke me up when she touched my hand.

She put the tea down and wrapped a soft blanket around my shoulders.

Touched my hand again and looked into my face. She smiled.

I saw Michael, she said, on the bridge.

I could smell smoke on the girl and would have loved a roll-up to go with the tea, but I'd left my tobacco on the boat. There was the river rot smell again and I realized it was coming from me and not anywhere else.

It's not like we're a single organism, the red-headed girl said.

Who was that terrible English painter whose red-headed girls looked like they were sleepwalking? Drippy-looking, as Nan would have said. Holman Hunt? This girl's bright eyes had dimmed to match the events of the day, but she was an electric presence. Burne-Jones, that's who it was. Red-haired girls on the stairs. Looking like they'd all been bashed on the head or doped.

While I was sleeping the girl had tied up the flame of her

hair, and there was a pattern, as I looked at her side on, made by the symmetry of the pulled-up hair at the back of her neck, and a rising line of separated freckles just above the neck of her T-shirt. The plain black T-shirt was different to the one she'd been wearing when she'd helped me bring John to the house. Dry.

Michael would have been a boy lost in the tall grass when he was with her, unable to see anything else.

What? I said.

Red padded away from the room. Head up, nose out. Searching for John.

You know, she said. The Kaplans. We're not like, one creature. With a single purpose. I'm not him. Don't put what he does on me.

Red came slowly back into the room hanging her head. I put my hands either side of her narrow ribcage. Could feel her heart beating against the tips of my fingers.

I know sweetheart, I said.

Death in every part of the room, in my hands, in air that was still fringed with the river damp that John Rose had carried with him everywhere.

You should see your face, Alexandra said.

You have an unfortunate mien Terry, Evelyn Crow had said to me once. Like the world's against you.

Michael's face said you'd pay for not seeing him, the girl said. Do you know what I mean? Set hard. People look at me and think of all the things I can't be, he said. Can't be an artist if I look like this, talk like this, come from where I come from. Mike was going to show them. It worked, she said. He disappeared and we're still talking about him.

I think my dad quite liked Mike, Alexandra said. Thought he was smart, which he was, a hard worker. Driven. Just didn't want him anywhere near me. But Mike was so dreamy there was never any chance of that.

What was he like? I said.

Michael was like a dark flower, she said.

I drank the hot sweet tea. Remembered she was not yet twenty.

When Mike was happy, his face would open up, like a flower in the sun. Big kissy lips. Big eyes, like his dad. It's also true that lots of times he was just a curly headed scowl who wouldn't say anything for hours.

I bet you were the sun coming out and going in, I thought but didn't say.

Mike was always making maps. Said he felt like a disinherited prince.

Alexandra looked at me.

Not literally, she said. You know about Perseis and her family?

No, I said, I don't really know anything.

So her family are minted, apparently. Richer than my dad. But they cut Perseis off when she took up with Gene.

She put a red strand back behind her ear.

Back then, the girl said, after I got to know Gene, I'd ask him how he was and he'd give me his naughty-boy grin – the same one Mike had – and he'd say he was happy as a fat spider. I remember he used to say that all the time.

I can't imagine Gene happy, I said.

I don't think he was though, she said, that's what I mean. Mike said his mum was always on at Gene. Nothing was good enough. Mike said he felt like two people. That he was being pulled in too many directions at once. Loved loved loved his dad, but had this glamorous mum who was always whispering in his ear. Telling him he was someone else.

Mike knew it would be fairly easy to make his mother's family love him, Alexandra said, the only grandson. And if he had money he could spend all his time drawing and painting. Plus they lived in Paris and Mike was desperate to see Paris, especially after Vesna died – you know about Vesna? – Mike was really upset. We talked about going to Paris together, I could pay for us, but he wouldn't do it. Said he wouldn't betray his dad.

Did Mike talk about Anthony Waters? I said. Do you know him?

I've known Tony Waters for as long as I can remember, she said, and I know almost nothing about him. Tony and my dad have secrets. They were arguing about somebody called Brady once and stopped talking when I came into the room. I try and stay out of his way.

Not like that, she said, looking at me. And not with me. Tony Waters only has eyes for Perseis. It could be sweet, right? And a bit sad. But it's not. Tony Waters gives me the whim-whams.

Red had crossed the room. The light in it had moved, and the dog lay stretched out and sleeping, talking in her sleep more than usual. What do you say to a broken-hearted dog?

My father didn't send me to Switzerland to be the same girl I was before I left, the girl said.

I looked at her.

Nobody said this to my face, she said, but I was sent away so I wouldn't talk. My dad didn't want the police asking questions about Tony and finding out things he didn't want them to find out. Secrets. So they got me out of the country and told the police shit about Gene instead. And who knows what Tony Waters told Perseis?

And I bet every time the police took Gene in, she said, Tony suddenly appeared at her door. I think Tony put my dad up to sending me away, if you want to know the truth. Which kind of makes me hate my dad. For being weak.

In Switzerland the other girls treated me like some tragic heroine, Alexandra said. But it was nothing like that. Michael said: I'm going for a swim, you coming? I said: too sleepy. Mike was pissed off. Gene and Perseis had a massive row. About money. Vesna wasn't there to talk to. I'm going to swim over the weir, Mike said. I dare you, I said, like, yeah, of course you are. I thought he was just talking. I had my eyes closed. I never even saw him go in the water. When I woke up I couldn't see him. Sometimes I think Mike isn't dead and that he just kept on swimming right off the island. That one day he's going to come back for me.

The girl looked at me.

I came back because Gene asked me, she said. I wrote to him, told him everything I knew about Mike and what happened. Gene sent me this long, long letter back. They're eating me alive here, he said, which is something Mike would say. I'm being eaten alive. At the bottom of the letter Gene had made a little drawing of a fat spider being eaten. They think I did it, he said. Nobody knows I didn't except you. Come back and tell them what you told me. And I did. Told my dad if he didn't bring me back he could forget about ever seeing me again.

Don't say what you're thinking, Alexandra said, looking suddenly angry. Mike didn't kill himself. The current was too strong, or he got tangled up or smashed into the weir. Don't even think what you're thinking. Not to me or Gene or Perseis or anybody else. Mike didn't kill himself. He didn't.

The girl's phone buzzed in her back pocket. She took it out and looked at it and made a face.

You better go, she said. My parents are on their way home.

I didn't want to leave her crying, but there were things I needed to do. Other people I needed to talk to.

Red, I said, wake up.

Go out the back way, the girl said.

The girl told me you tried to save him, Nancy Rose said from the riverbank.

Coming from the weir. Dressed all in black on a scorching day. Standing in shade under the tree where her father's departed goldfinches sang in the springtime.

I was in the open wheelhouse surrounded by salvaged wood and wire. A million years ago, I'd known an old woman named Pearl, who sold felt-tip colourings from her pitch outside a payday loan and money transfer place. Birds and fishes mostly, but other animals if she was feeling inspired, wolves and leopards, lambs and lions. Pearl made her pictures on pieces of stiff card, hardboard, the soft balsa-like wood of fruit boxes, and she made frames from found wire that she would bend to the wood or board. The old woman would arrange her pictures on an old, grey blanket, and sit on a turned-over crate, playing a kazoo and shaking her decorated money tin as people went by.

Ten days since John's death. The paintings were still up on the bridge, but except for an increase in the number of visitors to the island, nothing else had changed. September was coming and I needed money fast. I was fixing some of my best drawings onto scavenged card. Also made a dozen or so paintings directly onto hardboard. I remembered the poster of the missing girl, Gill, I'd seen the day I left the city, with its border of hearts and birds. I carved a printing block with a pattern as close to the remembered design as I could make it, and used the block to make borders on the pictures. Then I made frames from the salvaged wire. I thought I could set up a pitch outside the boatyard store, where the day-trippers and weekenders gathered to drink coffee before heading off into the forest or a walk along the towpath.

Weekends there were always people on the bridge, hanging over the sides to take selfies with the paintings. That seemed to be the extent of outside interest in the giant portraits. Several times I had seen Perseis in a dinghy before the bridge, looking up at Michael, Anthony Waters holding the little tender steady in the strong currents. One day I came back to the boat and found she had left me a new wildflower crown.

Recognized Nancy from her photograph, despite the extra weight she carried.

Close to my age. Fifty at least. Not a sightseer or a new boat owner thinking of settling on the island. Someone who might be a school head, a business person or even a police officer. A bulky, red-brown shoulder bag that did not match the rest of her outfit. Thought I could see the shape of shoe heels pushing against the fabric of the bag. I saw tight curls, under a plain black headscarf. Hips wider than her shoulders. Thick wrists and ankles. Beautiful hands, slender and manicured. She had her father's mask-like face, all set up to conceal. But like John Rose, strong feelings showed more clearly than I expect she thought they did.

She was only coming from one place.

Alexandra Kaplan was at the funeral? I said.

She seemed very upset, Nancy Rose said.

She lost her boyfriend in the river, couple of years ago.

She didn't tell me, Nancy said. The poor child.

I didn't know where the service had been held. Whether John Rose had been buried or cremated. I wasn't there. I didn't know anyone from the island who had been.

The last I saw of the old man was when the paramedics had refused to let me ride in the ambulance with him.

John's look of wonder, that's what I remembered. Because of something he'd seen at the end, or for what he suddenly felt happening to his heart, I didn't know. I didn't know if it was wonder at all.

Her father is Alex Kaplan, I said. He owns the island.

I'm aware, Nancy said.

She didn't know her father is trying to evict us, I said.

I'm going to try and help her, Nancy said. It was brave, what she did. She's finding out a lot of things at once. It's a shock.

Saw again the girl jumping into the boat like she was falling.

Your father was dead before I got to the dock, I said.

You tried, Nancy said.

After leaving Alexandra Kaplan, Red and I had got back into the Zodiac. Stayed out on the river. Didn't want to face the things I had to do, the people I had to tell. Spent most of that time looking at the paintings on the bridge. Kept thinking and I didn't want to think. Not about Mike or Waters or the Kaplans. Thinking made the pictures, the bridge and the river, completely disappear. Tried to keep the paintings in front of my eyes and the thoughts would rise up and make the pictures disappear again and I'd start over.

Like a man saying goodbye, John hadn't gone yet.

My hands warmed on the wheel. Made from some anti-corrosive metal alloy, rigid, with a tight protective covering of PVC. The layer was worn, faded, with a very slight give, and as my hands warmed the covering softened and gave a fraction more, and I could feel the places where John's hands had most often been, and I fit my own hands to those spaces. Believed I could feel the sweat and oil from his hands worn into the wheel.

The last time I saw Nan when she still knew who I was, I told her I loved her. Half a dozen things wrong with her and all of them could kill her. Didn't look after herself, eat, nothing. Just heroin. Now she was getting the shit for free. White hospice bed. Lost so much weight she looked like she was far away. Ancient-looking slits in her ears where the gold earrings had been taken out. I always said I loved her and she never said it back. I knew she loved me, but she never said so. Took me in. Didn't have to.

The nurse brought Nan the dinner choices on a slip of paper. Big meals full of carbohydrates, but easy to eat. Shepherd's pie, fish fingers and chips, trifle with extra custard. Tick a box for what you want. Nan tried to force the pen to the paper. Holding the pen wrong, the paper buckling in her hand. Making bird scratches on the paper. I remember my heart falling out of me. Exactly like that. Falling and falling.

That was when we both knew.

Death came into her eyes. Been hiding under her bed all this time. Now it was in there with her and she could feel it and touch it. Nan looked at me and she could tell I'd seen it to.

Do you want me to do that? I said.

No, she said, her voice thick.

She was always thirsty. I held the plastic beaker of juice. Put the straw in her mouth. Took it out, wiped her mouth.

She said she wanted me to write down something she would tell me. To be read out at the funeral.

I always think it's a shame that the main event's not there, she said.

She didn't go through with it. The idea that she would have to say her last words to me – so I could write them down or otherwise remember them – maybe that stopped her.

I could have asked her questions. About my mum and dad. Who were they and where did I come from? About Nan's people, the Goddens, and how long they had been in the south.

Farm labourers, train firemen, soldiers. What stories had my people told about themselves. Their rituals and special days. How they sounded when they sang.

Last chance, but questions would have hurt her. Felt disloyal.

I love you, I said instead.

Nan held out her arms.

I love you too, she said.

Pure contact. The back of her head fit into my hand.

I should have stayed with her, but I had to get out of there. I was only a kid.

When I came back to see her for the last time, she did not know who I or anybody else was, and she did not look human any more. I keep coming back to the colour yellow, when I think of her then. Breathing bones.

Nan's last words were known only to herself. The last words I heard her say were: I love you too.

Look after the blessed dog, John had said.

Looked down at Red. Panting in the thin shade of the Zodiac's inflated sides, big thick tongue flopped over her teeth.

I was almost out of fuel.

All right Red, I said, let's get you some water.

The sun high overhead. The boat wheel hot in my hand. The paintings on the bridge were shining. John Rose was doubly everywhere.

Came back to windhorse prayer flags and Jolly Rogers. Painted banners. Music coming from speakers in the trees. Set up for a feast. Fire pit. A party for the paintings. A victory.

The smile died on Stella's face when she saw me up close.

What's happened? she said. Where's John?

Hadn't asked John for his help, he wouldn't be dead. That's what I was thinking. Thought he was bulletproof. Didn't see him. Tired old man just about hanging on.

—

Red was sitting close to me, looking at Nancy Rose. Making indistinct noises every time Nancy spoke.

Your dog all right? Nancy Rose said.

That's Red, I said, she was your father's dog.

Nancy looked at me and then looked at the dog. Must have seemed like a marooned wild man, dirty, surrounded by broken wood and wire. The dog did look crazed, mouth open like that, eyes brightly staring. I tried not to say John's name when Red was around.

My father never had a dog in his life, she said.

Don't tell Red, I said. You'll want to see the boat.

I spent the best part of my childhood working on it, Nancy said. Weekends, school holidays when I wanted to be with my friends. Sanding until my fingers bled. Cuts, blisters. Dad kept us working when mum said to stop. Everything had to be done the way he wanted it done, or else. After I finally said no, I never wanted to see the damn boat again.

A dragonfly whirred across the space between us. Nancy stood with her back to the river that shone like stamped tin, doubling the boats and trees, the floating swans set in the water's shining embrace. Riverbank full of silver coins.

Nancy stepped aboard.

Lightly touched the paintwork at the threshold.

Wait there Red, I said.

The dog followed me in.

I watched Nancy take in the mould. Close enough to register lavender, clean sweat.

Nancy was looking at her graduation picture.

There should be some correspondence, she said, from my mother's care home. Do you know where he kept his letters?

Rough idea. Chair by the fire. Found it. Bag half full of papers. Handed it over.

She stuffed the papers into her shoulder bag.

Did my father owe any money? she said.

I'd be surprised, I said. More likely that people owed him money. Had to guess I'd say your father died owing nothing to anybody.

Nancy looked at me like I'd come down in the last shower.

You say that knowing nothing about me, she said.

I don't want to think badly of him, I said.

Then don't, she said. That's a luxury I don't have. He was the man you knew. I knew somebody else. Dad's own father was a tyrant. Tried to beat the Lord into him. Did he tell you anything of his childhood?

No, he talked about being a sailor.

Dad left Jamaica when he was just a boy, fifteen, Nancy said. Went to Chicago, alone, worked in the stockyards. He talked about the snow. How shocking it was . . . Did he tell you about prison?

No.

He got into trouble. A girl, a shooting.

After he got out he somehow made it to England. Joined the Merchant Navy. The blessed navy, she said, imitating her father's voice.

Red raised her head from John's chair.

Get out of there Red, I said.

She stayed where she was. Put her head down.

Do you know about the goldfinches? I said.

We hadn't spoken in years, she said.

I rubbed the porthole and pointed.

There's a colony of goldfinches living just there, in those trees, in the spring. Your father used to put down special seed, niger seed, every year, and that's why the goldfinches come back every spring to the same place. Who knows, it's a nice story.

I don't remember any goldfinches when I was a kid, Nancy said.

You have an idea what you want to do with the boat? I said. Somebody would give you something for her. For the paintwork at least.

I don't think so, she said.

I could see John up early in the dark freezing mornings, alone, clearing leaves and bird shit from the tarp, could smell the wine vinegar from the endless fight against the black mould that was blooming once more on the bulkhead. I could still feel his embrace, the steel wool and woodsmoke flavour of his old coat.

Why not? I said.

Nancy looked at me like I could waste my time but she wasn't going to let me waste hers.

I don't have the heart, she said. And I'm too busy.

Doing what? I said.

I'm a children's lawyer, she said. Beaten kids, abused kids. Runaways, addicts. Children in care, prison, psychiatric hospitals. Kids who are accused of crimes, who can't afford a lawyer. We don't make money. We rely on contributions.

There was a long strange time after Nan died, and I was out on my own, a runaway, sixteen, when I would dream that I'd killed somebody. Didn't matter where I slept. Park, doorway, sometimes an older woman's bed. Spent a summer under a pier. Waking inside the dream as a killer, a murderer on the run with this terrible secret I thought everyone could see. Trying to get to Nan's door and never making it before the cops grabbed me. A door that got knocked down pretty soon after I left to make way for a car park, so the place I was trying to get to no longer existed.

Are you all right, Mr Godden? Nancy said.

In the small, dark, moving space, portholes and other unknown openings, invisible gaps in the structure of the boat, allowed criss-crossing light rays of different dimensions to enter the cabin. Nancy stood looking at me from the centre of these golden bars, as if they were coming from her, and not the world outside.

Yes, I said. I'm all right.

I got what I came for, she said. You want the boat Terry, you're welcome to stay here.

She looked again at the mould-threatened photo of herself.

She took the picture from the wall, turned it over. Read something on the back that made her put her hand to her mouth. She put the picture into her shoulder bag with her father's papers. Looked around the boat once more.

I thought I would feel different when this day came, she said.

I'm very sorry, I said.

She went outside and I followed her broad outline across to my boat.

The small study I'd made of John, for the bridge paintings, was among the material I'd brought up to the wheelhouse. Thought I could make some copies of it to sell outside the boatyard store.

Wait a second, I said.

Grabbed the portrait, put it back in its bubble-wrap sleeve.

I made this of your dad, I said.

Nancy looked at the picture, gently touched the puffed-up plastic. Saw her go in her mind from what she was looking at, to the giant portraits on the bridge that she must have seen, but had not asked about.

It's amazing what you can do when you have so little to go on, Nancy said.

Is there somewhere I can reach you? I said.

Anthony Waters, or Brady Millar, wearing a red cotton thread around his wrist, put the keys under the counter.

The Red Thread was the name of a late-night drinker that came and went thirty years ago. Word of mouth. Couldn't tell you where it was. Greek bloke who ran it – called himself a poet, drank all day, died – said it was named for the thread Ariadne gave Theseus. To help him escape the labyrinth after killing the minotaur. Theseus later deserted her, and Ariadne died or ended up with somebody else. The minotaur was a prisoner in the labyrinth, that's what I remembered, like the bloke in the bar. He'd painted a load of red lines around the place that went nowhere.

You taking over the old man's boat? Waters said when I went into the boatyard store to take back Mrs Whitehead's keys.

You going to talk to me about moving in on what isn't mine? I said.

Man could smile. Bulletproof. Protected from the evil eye.

New quarter payments are due in a few weeks, he said. Whatever boat you're living on by then.

Just make sure she gets the keys, I said.

Left the boat as I found it. Full gas, firewood, bilges pumped.

Paid Waters for a big roll of rubbish sacks, and left.

Red waited outside.

Waters had set up a few picnic tables and Perseis, wearing a clean black apron, was bringing coffee to a young couple. She looked better. Saw me but don't think she remembered who I was. The thread around her wrist was older, a paler red.

The narrowboat was dark and cramped. Much smaller than the lifeboat. I missed the light in the wheelhouse, but that was all.

First day, in the galley, on two deep shelves behind a home-made curtain, I'd found a supply of tinned food and dried goods. Cans of sardines and pilchards, fish paste, corned beef, tinned tomatoes, kidney beans, hot pepper sauce, sacks of brown rice and red lentils. Chocolate powder, tins of peaches, condensed milk.

There was a short wave radio transmitter and a waterproof folder of emergency numbers and call signs.

A couple of hand-held fishing lines on their spools, an old tobacco tin full of old but rust-free hooks. Sat with John a few times when he was fishing.

What you after? I'd said to him.

Anything, the old man had said.

John kept a well-stocked tool box, and he had a battery radio, a bunch of chemical light sticks and a back-up Primus stove. Found a big, three-quarters full bottle of Johnnie Walker, which I wrapped up without looking at more than twice and put back where I found it.

Best of all, I found a fat, heavy, vacuum-sealed bag of coffee beans.

Gene had made himself scarce again, but he came to look at John's engine when I sent word through Adam.

You won't outrun the cops, he said, wiping his hands on a rag black with grease and oil, but she'll get you where you want to go.

Gene's hair was growing out, becoming downy, softening his death mask face but not by much. Burning eyes like black stars.

Dark clothes were dirty and slept in. Wolfed down the meal of corned beef and rice.

The police still hadn't put divers in the water as far as I could tell.

Fancy a coffee?

John's? Gene said. Point me at it.

Looking around. Almost hear him calling me a lucky bastard.

Stop here, I said, you want. Few days. Get it together.

Thanks, Gene said. Got too many bad habits.

I put the whisky bottle on the table. Gene poured some into his coffee. Looked at me. I shook my head.

You want to talk about it? I said.

Talk about what? Gene said. Glaring over his cup.

Gene helped me bag up rubbish. Worked fast or end up throwing nothing away. Kept a carved wooden box with no hinges.

John's photographs. Keepsakes. Discharge papers from

the merchant navy. Nearly thirteen years' service. Ancient first birthday card, brown paper, Little Bo-Peep. Faded blue bonnet, red ribbon. To dear little John. RHS certificates – first prize, runner beans, marrows. Second prize, onions, sets or autumn sown. Membership of the Royal Antediluvian Order of Buffaloes. Black and white photos of unknown people. Kept it all for Nancy.

Sometimes a name on the back. Cyril, Vi, Aunt Phyl. John and Vesna. John and baby Nancy. John Vesna Nancy. The red-brown box was hand carved with bodies, all crammed together, heads at strange angles, long arms and legs sticking into unhappy faces, no space between, packed in. Wasn't an expert but thought it was sandalwood.

Me and Gene went down to the building site carrying two big sacks of rubbish each. Had a dozen more sacks on the boat.

The contractors and work crew had been on the island for over a week. Building materials ferried upriver. Stacked in contraband shapes. Roped tarpaulin. Boots echoing as the men crossed the iron weir to the island, where a handful of defiant banners still rose and fell on river breezes in the honeyed light of September mornings.

A big blonde kid with stickers on his hard hat pushed a wheelbarrow. Gene used the skip without asking or talking, and walked away, carrying the sack I'd given him half-filled with tins of food, a twist of ground coffee. Nobody noticed him.

Shovels and kangoes breaking up the ground. The island

air thick with dust. The voices of happy men rising into the trees.

Making money with the sun on their backs, dreaming of a beach-bar getaway. Tinny background radio. Burst of a jackhammer drowning out the sing-a-long.

The fair kid said: Found all this in the mud, look.

There was a yellow rubber duck. A copper sheet containing what might have been Sanskrit for all I knew, or a different form of English. A rusted spear. Handful of keys. Black coins. Dipped into the wheelbarrow and pulled out a clay pipe with an unbroken stem. Tapped the bowl of the pipe against the flat of his other hand. The stem broke. The kid threw the pipe back into the wheelbarrow.

Came up with a small book with a leather cover stamped with a golden cross. To Dor, the boy read, with love and best wishes for your birthday, November fourth 1963, love Jack.

Give me the prayer book, said a Belfast voice I recognized. Skip the rest of the ackamarackus.

The Belfast man, wearing a high-vis jacket over a pale-blue shirt with the sleeves rolled to the elbow, was sat at a picnic table playing cards with a thin, hatchet-faced man. Hard hat upside down on the ground. Big freckled head, white corona of hair, big nose. Massive hands. The strap of his watch looked tight on his wrist. New blue supermarket jeans with a crease. Tan brogues. A big hard man all around.

The hatchet-faced man, a pencil behind his ear, said:

Gave the bloke the price for the scaffolding.

And? the Belfast man said, looking up from his cards.

Didn't even breathe hard, the hatchet-faced man said.

The Belfast man smiled, carried on playing cards. Kaluki, it looked like.

Couple of flasks on the table. Phones. Worn-looking Tupperware. The rescued prayer book with its hard maroon cover. Bits and pieces: slice of Bakewell tart, the core of a pear, an open packet of Smokey Bacon Taytos. A paring knife. Tobacco tins brought out. Fags rolled and lit. Blue smoke rising like signals.

McNab. That was his name. Liked to hear himself talk. Skin a foot thick. Looked after his lads. Knew how to squeeze a profit out of the most tightly priced jobs. Recognized the hatchet-faced man too, but couldn't remember his name.

Hello McNab, I said.

Terry Godden? McNab said. I heard you were dead.

Not yet.

You didn't go to Tahiti? Live under the banana trees?

Not lately, I said. Borrow your skip?

Not a bother, McNab said, work away.

The hatchet-faced man looked at me as I threw my rubbish bags into the skip. Glossy black hair the most impressive thing about him. Kept it a little too long for his age. Swept back. Stuff in it to make it shine and keep it in place. Eyes the colour of muddy water. Too close together. Brick-red face. Not all from the sun.

The hand was over. The man took the pencil from behind his ear, licked the end and totted up the value of the cards that were left.

McNab said: That's a good dog. None better.

The hatchet-faced man finished counting. He cut a piece of pear with the knife and held it out to Red.

Here girl, he said.

Stay where you are, I said.

Red looked up at me in disbelief and lay down with her head between her paws, her sunset-orange eyes fixed on the pear. Sighed like a girl in a posh book. The hatchet-faced man ate the piece of fruit and said nothing. Looking at me.

McNab was quiet for a moment. I could hear Red panting.

The lads tell me you're the fellow made the big paintings, he said.

Had some help, I said.

You're not working then?

That what you're doing, I said, looking at the food-littered table. Working?

I'm overseeing operations, McNab said. The whole scheme would come crashing down without me, so it would. You live here Terry, or are you just passing through?

I live here.

And it's a grand spot, McNab said.

Yes, I said.

I can see you've taken to it, McNab said. Like one of those fellows who lives in the trees, he said. Your man Swampy.

I don't know what you're talking about, I said.

You always were a sensitive man Terry.

I'll see you around McNab.

McNab looked at me with clear blue eyes.

You wouldn't by any chance be a fifth columnist Terry? he said.

A what?

A saboteur?

Not me, I said.

Ah well, McNab said.

The workmen left before dark, replaced by two security men, who had set up in the timber and plasterboard hut the workmen had built for them. Big men. Shoulders up by their earholes. Tougher than a goat's knee. The workmen had also built a fenced pen. I watched the guards in black uniforms unload two large German shepherd dogs from a van with Kaplan Security written on the side, and march them onto the island.

They crossed the weir above the painted islanders. Big black and tan dogs, wearing harnesses so that they made a soft chinking sound when they walked, with the sloping backs German shepherds have. Straight front legs and hind legs bent almost in a crouch, like they were always ready to leap at your throat.

Red had her back up the whole time the dogs were in sight, making a low, drawn-out growl that did not break, but repeated itself in waves until the dogs passed from view.

Meaner than a junkyard dog, I said, and praised her until she smiled.

The islanders gathered inside a ring of head-high lanterns, hooked by wire in the trees.

A place neither light nor dark, made changeable by the power of the breeze to redirect each paper lantern's golden cast.

I stood at the edge of the meeting, just beyond the light.

Red sat still by my feet, Guarding the sack of food.

The leaves, though coloured bronze and gold, had not begun to fall. The air remained full of fragrance from the cooling ground. A flowering edge to the permanent funk of damp. There was the faintest of cold bites against the skin.

People stood talking, or sat on old patterned blankets, on camp chairs with rusted legs. Some wearing warm clothes, hoodies and windbreakers. For others it was still summer in the mind. I wasn't wearing a jacket, but I'd been collecting firewood for days. Up towards the camp, in the darkening sky above the treeline, I saw the darker line of woodsmoke.

Stella across the clearing. Gaunt with her hair tied back. Work, the kid, the cause. No money and soon no home. Heavy uncertainty. Pressing down. Red red eyes. Mouth a straight slash across her face.

Danny was standing in front of his mother, wearing a

wheat-coloured cord jacket, hard-eyed and pissed off. Stella had her arms crossed over the boy's chest. She'd aged ten years since I'd arrived on the island, and Danny was now up to her shoulder. The boy's hair had grown long, and was the brightest point in the uncertain light.

Stella waved one-handed. Signed at me, two fingers pointed at my eyes, then pointed at Danny behind his back, then pointing at herself. Making the talking sign.

Gave her the thumbs up. Stella said something to the boy and kissed him. Danny came over rubbing his cheek. Red stood up and wagged her tail. The boy ruffled the dog's ears.

Danny nodded at the sack of tins of food at my feet.

You taking those up there? he said.

Now that the guards and dogs had arrived, rumours were strong that the bailiffs and cops were coming to clear the camp.

Sometimes rumours are all you have. If I thought McNab would tell me anything I'd have asked him.

Said he won't come down, I said to Danny. Said he needs to be there.

I'll go, the boy said.

I put my hand on the boy's chest. Heart beating fast.

I need you to do something else, I said.

Between the high tree tops, stars showed in a new denim sky. Water sparkled at the edge of the forest.

Put this on, I said, and pulled out John's old beanie and gave it to the boy.

It smells, he said.

Tuck your hair in, that's it. Circle round. Don't let any-body see you. Make sure the people at this meeting are all supposed to be here. No strangers. Come back when you're done and tell me what you saw.

What do I do if I see someone I don't know?

Nothing, I said. You don't go near them, understand? Try and remember something about them. The most important thing is that nobody sees you. Got it?

Got it.

Good man, I said.

The boy took off into the trees, and with John's dark hat on, disappeared.

Red, I said, and the dog ran after him.

Safe enough.

Stella moved to the centre of the crowd.

Faces set and waxy in the unreliable lantern light. Voices rumbling and getting louder. Atmosphere thick. Headaches, teeth crumbling. Taste of blood and acid in the mouth. Fear humming on a shared frequency, moving thickly in an end-less loop I could almost see. Food or rent, rent or food. These were our choices. Even if you had been born and lived with this danger, when the sharp point came it was new every time.

Dogs slept humped on the ground, not caring. Standing figures shouted. Arms windmilling. Casting outsized shad-ows. Groups of figures sat together.

Like one of those big historical paintings. National Gal-lery. A tribe gathered in the traditional meeting place. The camp by the river. The water painted in lines of navy and silver between the trees. A returned scout is telling the news. Standing while the others sit. Arms spread. A look of dread on his face. An army of strange soldiers is coming. The scout points as he speaks. White topsails in the distance.

You look at the painting and read the little card and you think, I've never heard of the such and such tribe. I wonder what happened to them? Near the museum and the shopping centre and the towers built on the land where the tribe once lived there will be places named after their defeated war chiefs and politicians. Crossroads and government buildings. Dark people sleep on hard benches in a park named after their great leader, waiting for the cops to move them on.

We need to protect the most vulnerable among us, Stella said. That means none of us pay the increase, even if you're able. Just give it a few more days. There are people out there on our side.

Kaplan's not going to back down, a man standing in the half-light, Tuppy Lawrence, said. Even John Rose knew that, rest his soul.

John did know that, Stella said over the shouts. Why he said to stand together.

The life had gone out of the protest with John's death.

I'm going to pay, Goldie's dad said, and I know for a fact others will too. The new shower block is worth the money. Frankly I'm glad to pay if it means getting rid of the spongers and troublemakers. There's people who don't belong here. Those people in the camp. They're nothing but squatters.

We need to oppose the increase for all our neighbours who can't afford it, Stella shouted over the noise. Kaplan can't throw us all off!

Face it Stella, Tuppy said. The fees have gone up, and they're not coming back down. The men have started work. The law's on his side. We're getting notices to pay or get out. The courts ruled in his favour. It's over. There's nothing we can do about it. It'll be winter soon. You want to think about what's best for your boy. Not go around stirring people up for a fight they can't win.

There was a kind of snarling at Tuppy's words, that may have come from Stella, or another of the women in the crowd.

Terry! somebody shouted.

Red loped towards me out of the dark, mouth open. Danny running close behind. Almost didn't recognize the boy. Danny stopped and doubled over, breathing hard.

What are you going to do when the fees go up again, Tuppy? Stella asked. Which they will. And everybody you know who might have helped you has already been kicked out?

Terry, somebody called out again. What do you think?

Danny, still bent over, spat and then raised his head.

Pointed downstream, where the lights of a low flying helicopter flashed above the river. The helicopter banked left and high at the island. Coming for us. Then we were underneath it, the machine roaring. I covered Red's ears.

The air became almost solid with bronze and golden leaves that still did not fall, but swirled in loose and fast-moving gigantic wreaths. The leaves stung when they hit. People ran for shelter. Unlighted lanterns whole and broken were flying through the air.

The helicopter thumped towards the camp.

Danny raced ahead into the trees.

Danny! I shouted, but the boy couldn't hear me.

Pulled up fenceposts littered the path through the forest. Cut fencing. There were broken signs saying No Trespassing. Private Property. The dry tracks of machines.

Red ran to her family and the dogs milled around, going nowhere.

Adam was sitting bare-chested on a camp chair. The helicopter thumped above us, bending the tops of the trees and making the dogs' hair swirl and stand on end.

Nina stood behind Adam, braiding his hair. The girl's mouth full of the green plastic bands that she was using to tie off each completed braid. Somebody had used a marker pen to embroider the huge livid scar on Adam's chest with a green geometric pattern, abstract ferns and leaves. Adam's fingernails were painted a brilliant shade of green, the varnish bottle sticking out the back pocket of Nina's jeans. Between Adam's feet were coils of wire that he was systematically cutting into sections.

Had to shout to be heard.

Hell of a time to be sitting around, I said.

Adam, trance-like, didn't answer.

All right Paul? Jason shouted.

The gnomic man was surrounded by a pile of torn-apart cardboard boxes. Consignments to the contractors. Pipes. Toilet bowls. Jason was using a length of cut wire to strap a thick piece of cardboard to his left shin, knee to ankle. Working fast. Jason's right leg was already protected. There were arm guards on his forearms, wrist to elbow, and a large cardboard breastplate that he'd padded with what looked like plastic packing.

The hollowed-out tree Gloster Vince slept in was abandoned and there was no sign of him. The sharpened punji fence around his camp had been taken out of the ground and the sticks scattered all around.

Vince has upped sticks Paul! Jason shouted.

Why don't you clear out? I shouted to Adam.

Adam's green eyes suddenly focused and lasered into me.

Where to? he shouted back.

Paul! Jason shouted. Whoever heard of anybody owning a forest? Where'd he get it from? And where did the bloke he got it from get it from? You ever ask yourself that Paul? Paul! Listen! Some rich fucker got a bunch of poor fuckers to kill another lot of poor fuckers, for a richer fucker, and the richer fucker gave the rich fucker some more land, and made the rich fucker fucking richer. Stole the fucking country. Talk about a piss-take! It's all in the fucking Domesday book Paul. Paul!

I looked at Danny among the frightened dogs. I grabbed him, cupped my hand to his ear.

Stay out of sight, I shouted.

The dogs went crazy.

A ragged line of torches burst from the trees, criss-crossing beams moving crazily.

Shouting black figures charged into the clearing. Police and security guards and two others with hi-vis jackets, carrying long poles with nooses on the end. Gloved, masked, the fucking visors, flak jackets. Figure in a white helmet, the bailiff, directing. Giving orders. Masked figures dragged a big cage into the clearing, the metal wire chinking. Flashes travelled up and down the meshing as the cage caught the starlight. Inside the cage was dark as absence.

Bailiff read out a notice nobody could hear. Before he was finished the cops and guards began tearing down the shelters and wickiups, crushing belongings. Swiping at the dogs who lunged at them with snapping jaws. Forcing dogs into the cage. The helicopter above, recording everything. A noose flashed silver as a figure with a catchpole lunged at Red.

Nina jumped on the back of one of the police. She yanked his visor up and tipped something in the cop's face. The cop ran into a tree, trying to smash the girl against it. Nina held fast. Her mouth was open and I knew she was yelling all the time. The cop threw her onto the ground where she bucked and struggled as he twisted her arms round and tied her wrists with plastic handcuffs.

Dogcatcher caught Red in the stainless steel noose and pulled it tight, lifting her off the ground and into the air, twisting and kicking.

I charged at the dogcatcher and was smashed to the

ground. Tasted dirt. Rolled over. Stars in the sky. High above me the light of the helicopter, the rotor blades ka-chunk ka-chunk ka-chunking in my head. I couldn't hear anything else.

Danny came silently running. Crouched down. From the ground he looked like a small giant, carrying the night sky on his back. My mouth wouldn't work. Tasted blood.

Paul!

Jason's voice cut through the machine noise that had taken over my head.

Paul!

Got to my knees. Grabbed Danny. Held him. Pulled him back into the trees.

Jason charged in his cardboard armour. Took the dog-catcher off at the knees. Sat on top of him and started punching him in the face.

Bloke still had hold of the catchpole. Red still in the noose, but on the ground.

Found my voice.

Jason! The dogs!

Kept punching until the bloke was still.

Jason ripped the catchpole from his hand and found the mechanism that opened the noose.

Red stood. Shaky, uncertain. Walked in a half circle. Jason threw the pole into the trees. Released the other dogs from the cage and led them into the trees. Nina, still hand-cuffed, had disappeared.

Red! Red! I called.

Red! Danny shouted.

Red, wobbly, turning this way and that, finally came to me. Mouth open and panting hard. Scared. Her heart thumped against my hand.

It's all right sweetheart, I said.

Terry, Danny said.

Adam had been fighting all the time so we could escape.

Now the giant youth was on his knees. To me he seemed to be rising out of the ground, not being beaten down to it by the guards and cops. They pinned his arms to his sides and forced his hands behind his back and handcuffed him. The bastards knocked him over. Then hauled him back to his feet. Adam didn't make a sound. Kept his head up and still, looking to where we were hiding in the darkness. Moving fast, Adam stuck out his elbows and spun in place, knocking a cop over.

Down on one knee, the cop drew a long baton.

Hold that fucker still, he said, and raised his stick.

Nothing I could do to help that wouldn't get me and Danny taken down with him.

Adam's screams followed me through the forest.

Red growled softly then gave a tiny warning yip.

Just enough for me to open my eyes. Still getting used to John's boat in the dark. The night was moon-soaked, and I woke to luminous shifting pools and splashes, where the silver-blue light penetrated the boat.

Soft knocking.

Not the cops. Cops had no idea of who I was. And they'd kick the door in. Not Adam. Stella had tried to find out where he'd been taken and got nowhere. Hard to make him disappear, Stella said, but I knew better. I saw Adam hand-cuffed and alone in the vast over-lit walkways of an unlisted secure unit. Everything that was his taken away. Boots for paper slippers. Bright green make-up roughly wiped away. The green bands taken from his hair. Even the braids that had been made with love were removed. Not before he was photographed, because his decorations made Adam look mad to the cops and doctors, and justified everything they did to him.

Adam wouldn't had given his real name but they'd find out who he was soon enough. Somebody will see the burns on his chest and look him up. Somewhere there'll be a file on him thick as a bible.

Adam as much as told me that he'd escaped from

wherever he was before. They wouldn't let him go this time. Adam was back where he belonged. Warehoused.

The graffiti had appeared overnight: *Free Adam, The Giant Rules, OK*.

Another soft knock. Red sat up. Moved her head to one side like a dog in a cartoon. Should have been trying to get through the door to see who was on the other side. Anxious. Didn't like loud noises or being alone. Scared of figures coming out of the dark.

Another knock on the side of the boat. Harder. Red barked once, sharply. I reached down for John's lump hammer that I kept by the side of the narrow cot which was too small for me and Red but she slept in it anyway.

Terry!

A young voice.

Who is it?

Goldie.

Goldie?

The girl was wide-eyed and silver-edged in the moonlight.

Grown since the winter. Up to my shoulder. She was all angles, her body still catching up with her height. Trackies and a hooded sweatshirt with a bumblebee on it: *Bee Nice*. Gold-blonde hair stuffed into the hood. Feet jammed into unlaced boots.

My dad's like, stay here, she said, but it's Danny, I can hear them shouting.

Locked Red in and went with the girl. Goldie reached

for my hand, the warm contact electric. Goldie looked at me, pushing a blonde curl back under her hood.

There were angry voices coming from Stella's boat. Goldie looked scared.

It'll be all right, I said. Go back.

McNab and his hard-faced offsider, whose name I could not remember, were standing over Stella.

Black shadows made the bulkheads darkly fluid.

A dog-boy with Danny's blonde head and Choo-Choo's long furry legs was partly visible through the crowd. Crammed into a corner.

Get out of here, I said.

Are you a man of influence now Terry? McNab said.

The big man looking bigger in the small space. Stella held herself tight, her hands and arms invisible inside a cardigan that looked wrapped around her twice. Could feel vibrations coming from her as McNab threw his weight around. Mental force pushing back. The men had been drinking. Alcohol bloomed in the too-small space, and I was back in all the old places. Men and drink racing each other to the prize of violence.

You need to leave, I said. Any harm comes to these people you won't get off this island.

McNab pointed a big finger at me.

I can fucking assure you, he said, that if you touch so much as a hair on our heads during these negotiations, every craft on this stretch of river will be a smoking ruin in the morning.

Don't swear in front of my son, Stella said.

McNab held up his hands.

Lo siento, señora, he said.

Closed his hands except for the finger he'd used to point at me.

But I speak the truth Terry, he said. Before the sun finds his hat.

What do you want McNab?

A word with the boy's father, he said.

Not got one, Danny said.

Danny, Stella said.

The boy's a volunteer Terry, McNab said. A young bandito. We caught him red-handed, smashing up a new consignment of pipes, the delivery note was still warm.

Did you do this? Stella said.

I never! Danny said, he's lying!

Choo-Choo barked.

What we'd like to know from young Danny, McNab said, is the identity of the boy with him. Who got away. The red-headed lad in the baseball cap.

Danny gave a small smile and held the dog tighter.

Told you, he said, I was on my own.

You think this is funny son? McNab said. I know you're lying to me.

Fuck off baldy! Danny said, arms folded.

Danny! Stella said.

Let me tell you a wee thing, McNab roared. You're lucky we're not at home, else your ma would be looking for your kneecaps. Keep a civil tongue in your head or I'll pull your arms off.

That's enough, I said.

I'm trying to keep the lad from durance vile, McNab said. I should really hand him over to the cops.

You wouldn't be here if you were going to get the cops involved, I said. Tell us what you want.

The hatchet-faced man leaned into the foreman and said something, his thin mouth barely moving. Leaned the other way so he was back where he was. Examined the end of his roll-up. Put it back in his mouth.

This boy's cost me money Terry, McNab said. Money I can't afford to lose.

McNab spread his hands.

The pair of us have been called out of our beds to find a solution, he said.

You'll find no money here, Stella said. I want you off my boat. Now.

I'll be your painter, I said.

McNab looked at me and smiled.

I've no painting jobs, he said.

You will have, in a few weeks.

Terry, would it surprise you to know I've thought of that already? I've the lads on notice.

I'll do it for less.

You'll do it for nothing, he said.

No McNab, I said, I won't do it for nothing. I'll do it for less.

And young Che here will stay out of my business?

Yes he will, Stella said.

I need to hear him say it.

Danny glared at his mother. Stella broke his stare and the boy looked down.

All right, he said.

All right what? McNab said. There's nothing all right about it. I'll not have the lads go short Terry.

It'll have to do, Stella said.

McNab looked at me.

You heard her, I said.

And the accomplice Terry, what am I to do about him?

The boy was on his own, I said.

Are you calling me a liar?

We'll take care of it, Stella said.

I have your word?

For God's sake McNab, I said.

Danny watching. Just his head moving. Paint on his hands.

McNab looked at the hatchet-faced man, who looked at me hard. Eventually he nodded.

Grand, McNab said, that's settled. Have you any drink in the house, to seal the bargain?

There's no drink, Stella said.

What about you Terry? McNab said. You were known to keep a bottle about your person.

The bar's closed, I said. Time you were going,

The hatchet-faced man looked at Danny as he was leaving.

Pointed an imaginary gun at him.

Danny looked at him with wide eyes.

Don't come back, I said.

The man put his fingers away, and he and McNab left.

Stella stood with the flat of her left hand raised, her mouth set hard in the way that was now familiar. Looking down. Stella's body tried to march, but the boat wasn't big enough. She ended up pacing in a tight circle, taking a couple of quick, shortened steps, then turning and coming back.

Was this her idea? she said at last.

Who? Danny said.

Stella raised her head and made a grunting sound like a bitten-off scream. She twisted her body so that she was leaning over her son.

Was it her idea? she said.

No! Danny shouted.

I don't believe you, Stella said.

Mum!

You keep away from her, Stella said.

Mum!

Do you hear me?

I'm just trying to help! Danny shouted, Jee-sus.

This is not the way, I said.

You got a better idea? Danny said. You want me to let them do to me what they did to Adam?

I looked at him. Blonde hair dark with sweat at the ends. Bottom lip stuck out. Super angry but scared too. Looking at me like I'd turned traitor.

I don't have any answers, I said, but McNab's not the problem.

Fucking talking, the boy said, fucking arguing. Mike was

right. Nobody listens, nothing changes. Nobody listened to you when Dad beat you up, and nobody's listening to you now.

Danny, I said.

You want somebody to pay attention, the boy said, you got to smash their shit up.

Where are you going? Stella said.

Nowhere!

Choo-Choo stood up at the word.

You stay away from her! Stella said, as the boy and the dog left the barge.

Danny! she shouted, do you hear me?

That's not my name! the boy yelled from outside the boat. Stella looked up at the bulkhead, took in a deep breath. Held it. Let it out finally. Looked at me.

The little bitch, she said. I felt sorry for her. What's she playing at? He gets arrested, for anything, he'll be taken away from me.

You don't know that.

Yes Terry, she said. I do. You don't know what you're talking about.

The famous gallerist said he hadn't been so excited by an untrained, self-taught artist for years. 'It's like Godden came straight from a life of addiction and sleeping rough with these wonderful paintings,' Crow said. 'Raw, unschooled. I don't understand why he'd go after his benefactor with an axe. I suppose Terry couldn't leave behind where he'd come from. People from disadvantaged backgrounds often can't. It's really a great shame, but I was in fear of my life.'

Found a newspaper account of my confrontation with Evelyn Crow inside a folder of drawings.

The headline – *Hate Gallery!*

Sat reading it on the small sun-washed deck. The gentle rise and fall. Muted hollow wood sounds.

Raw. Unschooled. Code words for no technique. Don't know what you're doing. Honest, that was another favourite. Searingly honest.

But. Who else was interested?

Sir Evelyn declined to comment specifically on the dispute, which Godden claims has left the gallerist in possession of his major work.

'I want to see what Terry is working on now,' Sir Evelyn said. 'I've almost forgotten about our incident. It's really not significant. It's become a kind of urban myth. Though we mustn't forget that potentially Terry remains very dangerous.'

Red appeared from out of the forest. Panting. Burrs stuck in her fur.

When she saw me she lifted her chin and made the soft questioning noise that sometimes made me believe she was going to start talking.

Have you read this shit? I said to her.

Red barged through the small space between my arms and legs, stepping on me, her hot flank rubbing across my face and leaving fur in my mouth. Went to her bowl and drank noisily, dripping water. She flumped down on the deck. Heavy exhaled breath.

Make yourself comfortable chum, I said, picking hair out of my mouth.

Red raised her head and sneezed, making her ears flap.

You OK? I said.

Red licked my hand.

Sun on my face, the rest of me in shade.

Turned the old Nokia on and lifted it towards the sky. In the warm air the skin on my hand and arm was sun dark.

Evelyn Crow Evelyn Crow Evelyn Crow.

Could hear John Rose talking as he poured whisky in his coffee: Grease the wheels.

Pressed call. Instant pick-up. A woman gave a name I couldn't hear. I could picture the clean walls of the gallery. The light from the high windows falling just so on the canvasses. Through those hushed rooms, an ordinary speaking voice would travel. If you were to shout, as I knew, it would sound like a series of explosions.

Evelyn Crow please.

Sir Evelyn is not . . .

Tell him it's Terry, I said. I'll wait.

I could hear noise from the site. Skill saws and angle grinders. Raised voices. Radios.

Terry, Evelyn Crow said, is that you?

I've got something for you, I said. Something you need to see. There's money in it. I'm not fooling around.

Well well, Crow said.

Hungry when I finished the call. There was a box of broken biscuits somewhere.

Sweet biscuit on my tongue. Stroking the dog. Really feeling the shape of her head under my hand.

Red licked my fingers. Carried on after she'd got all the crumbs.

I ate another golden biscuit.

Red followed my hand.

Then I called Nancy Rose.

We talked for a long time.

Nancy listened, and asked questions, and then she talked and I listened. I got her to repeat certain instructions.

Everything depends on Crow, I said.

Do you think he'll go for it? Nancy said.

The bug Red had blown out of her nose and onto the deck stood up and shakily walked away on the wet deck that must have seemed like a flooded new world.

I honestly don't know, I said. What about Adam?

I'll see what I can do, Nancy said, but don't get your hopes up.

Not likely, I said.

The night before Evelyn Crow came to the island, spots of what I thought were blood appeared on my bedclothes. More all over the boat. If I had been drinking I'd suspect myself. Found Red licking at herself and scratching at the door, mewling and barking to get out, and realized she was in season.

You seem concerned Terry, Crow shouted into the wind we made.

I didn't answer.

Had to lock her up. What state would the boat be in when I finally got back? Not just the spotting. Red had been fighting mad when I left, and I'd be gone for hours. Could she dig through wood planks?

Crow was summer-burned. A deep tan. Different man. Grown his hair out. Pushed back on his head in frozen white waves that did not move even in the speeding Zodiac. Fig and mint no longer. Some harsher citrus scent. There was a thin line of familiar snowy skin at his hairline, so that Crow's tan face looked like a rejuvenating mask. Pale blue shirt with an extra button undone. Khaki jacket. Khaki trousers tucked into brand new jungle boots.

Massive, almost square dark glasses. Gold watch. A Canon 5D Mark II camera on a strap over his shoulder.

Danny, in John's hat and a baggy sweatshirt, was staring at the young woman he was sat next to on the transom.

Laurel Archer, Crow had said, she's Burke's goddaughter. She's an admirer.

Long straight golden hair. A suntan she looked like she was born with. White teeth. Hazel eyes examined me until I looked away. Like I'd come wild out of the forest with drawings and paintings. Wasn't scared. Waiting to see what I would do.

Army green T-shirt with *Namaste, Bitches!* printed in pink lettering. Camouflage trousers with lots of pockets.

In the boat Laurel didn't want to let go of her coffee cup. Kept bringing it to her mouth long after it must have been empty. *Laurel* was written on the cup in black marker. Starbucks Starbucks Starbucks Laurel Starbucks. When she raised her arm a lot of fabric and plastic bracelets moved from her wrist to her elbow. Then she would hold the cup in her other hand and shake the bracelets back down to her wrist.

Laurel's mother, Crow said, shouting to make himself heard, knew Ariel. They were great friends.

Standing next to me in the bow. Keeping his balance. Conspicuously not holding on.

If he was worried she could hear him talking about her he didn't show it.

I must say Terry, this charming ville seems to suit you. I remember finding you in those dreadful rooms.

You didn't get that tan in England, I said.

You haven't heard, Crow said.

About what?

Dear Burke Damis has died. The poor man's heart gave out.

You've been in California?

You didn't know? Crow said. You really have cut yourself off from the real world. We can use that.

Some rich painter dying in California isn't the real world, I said.

There were still protest banners among the trees and flying from the boats, including one that just said: *Get Out*.

The death of a great artist is always an historical event, Crow said. In Burke's case of course there's a significant estate, the dispensation of which will change lives.

You're not safe there, I said.

Slack water. The hour before the tide turned.

The river was flat calm, but fast as I was going, the fragile dinghy sometimes lifted off the surface and skimmed or bumped over the water. I was pushing the Zodiac because I could, but I also hoped it would give Crow the shits.

As we flashed by, the trees and water were a display of golden light in fleeting patterns.

You need to sit down, I said. I have to stop or turn fast you'll be thrown out.

Crow leaned in close and shouted.

I'll take my chances.

The citrus scent was some kind of insect repellent.

You know, Crow said, Burke always understood that one must keep one's name before the public. Good or bad, doesn't matter. They mustn't be allowed to forget you,

233

Terry, no matter what. That way, they'll buy anything you sell them.

Even if it's shit, I said.

Crow flapped his hand like he was waving goodbye.

I need to know you understand Terry, he said. I don't always want to be looking over my shoulder. You're very much like Burke. You both hunger for the attention. I've always been grateful I'm not like that.

She here for insurance? I said. Case I shoot you, leave your body in the forest?

Crow turned to look at Laurel, talking to Danny on the transom.

Laurel Archer is a very rich young woman as of her godfather's passing, he said. And she likes your work. What she's seen of it.

Bet she's seen more of it than I have, I said.

The girl's astute, Crow said. She made herself helpful to Burke when others had forgotten him, he said. Burke took it into his mind that he'd failed, and that stopped his hand. He could be a difficult man. Laurel made him smile.

Damis couldn't paint? I said.

You also fear being unable to work? he said. Well, in Burke's case it made for horror. For him, and anyone who came near him.

Crow was looking at me so that I could see myself doubly reflected in his outsized sunglasses, surrounded by shining water.

The point is you couldn't get arrested, Terry, he said, tapping my arm. Nobody significant was interested in our show or your paintings. I'm sorry if I hurt your feelings. I was trying to generate traction against the day your notoriety would pay off. I'm very much hoping that starts today.

I could always get arrested, I said.

I wasn't trying to be clever, Crow said. The truth is I've been waiting for your call. I can't lie.

I cut the engine without warning and wrenched the wheel round. A dancing skirt of water rose and dissolved. Crow lost his balance and sat down hard on the inflated side of the boat, his hands palm down either side of him for balance. The boat drifted side on in the dark water that was the shadow of the bridge.

We're here, I said.

The kids had followed Crow from the minute he'd set foot on the island. Never seen anything like him. Laughing at his hair (Oi! Ice-cream head!), and clothes, the thin length and height of him (Oi! What's the weather like up there!). Kids hiding behind trees and looking in and sniggering at him through the boatyard store windows. Crow must have known he was being laughed at.

Show you round, I'd said, before we go look at the paintings.

Crow snapped away. Laurel filmed everything on her phone. Didn't ask anybody if it was all right.

A small crowd had gathered at the sight of Crow's camera, and were crowding into the shop.

A sallow young man with a scowl, holding hands with a

blonde girl who was taller than he was, said: Why is she filming you?

He's a painter, Crow said.

A what?

A painter.

Are you famous?

My name is Sir Evelyn Crow, Crow said. I am Mr Terry Godden's representative. Remember the name.

Waters looked at me like I'd grown another head.

What kind of painter? the scowling boy asked. Angry. At me, the girl, everything. He had a paperback, title out, in the pocket of his blue canvas jacket. *Lord Jim*. The girl's face told me the boy was getting ready to pick an argument.

Two coats, I said, one afternoon.

It was an old joke, but first the girl laughed, and then the boy.

I know that man, Crow had said when we were leaving the boatyard.

Who, the boy?

No, Crow said, putting his sunglasses back on, the chandler.

You follow the fights? I'd said.

Choo-Choo came charging fast around the corner and almost crashed into Crow. Danny came chasing after the deerhound.

Sorry I'm late, he said.

Looked at Laurel and gulped. Red in the face already.

You're here now, I said.

Danny's my crewman, I said to Crow. Plus he knows

more about the island than I do. You'll need to pay him. Hey Danny, no room for dogs this trip.

Danny said something I couldn't hear to the deerhound. The dog walked away and then stopped and looked back over its shoulder.

Go back Choo-Choo! Danny said, go back!

The big tall dog seemed to gather herself up before exploding into a hooping run and disappearing.

The fights? Crow said as we went into the forest. No. That man works for Alex Kaplan, surely?

How well do you know Kaplan?

Alex has bought some paintings from me over the years, Crow said. A man smart enough to take my advice.

In the dappled clearing near Michael's stones the trees were full of little pictures and mobiles chiming and swinging in the wind.

Below the branch, one of Michael's woodcuts swung back and forth.

Tell me about this, Crow said.

He was your friend, I said to Danny.

Danny put his finger on Michael's woodcut so that it stopped moving. Looked Crow up and down. Glanced sideways at Laurel, blushed.

I don't want to talk about that, he said. You wouldn't understand.

Yes, well frankly I'd like to see what we came all this way to look at Terry, Crow said, looking at his big watch. Sorry if that seems a bit brusque.

Don't you want to know what's happening here? I

said. It's all connected. This place, the kids, Michael, what happened to him, the fight to save homes, the paintings, everything.

I'd like to hear about it, Laurel said.

Are you recording this?

She nodded and looked down at the screen of her phone.

Tell us what's happening here, she said.

This community is under threat from an owner who wants to redevelop the island at our expense, I said, and then kick us off.

You've lived here a long time? Laurel said into the phone.

Crow had begun taking photographs.

I haven't lived here long – a year – so really I'm an outsider, I said. Sometimes that's even better though as people want to tell you how it is, if you're not trying to take the place over. People just want to live without being worried their homes will be taken away. It's pretty fundamental. I'm not new to this kind of place, or the kind of process that's happening here. I've heard it called social cleansing. It happened to my people, where I come from.

Danny had disappeared into the trees when Crow had started taking photographs.

Anyway, I said, you'll see.

Totally, Laurel said.

Crow slapped the back of his neck with an open hand.

If it's not too much trouble, Terry, Crow said. The paintings.

I was willing to bet he'd seen the pictures already and was already making plans, but I went along with him.

Don't take pictures when the kid's around, I said.

Why ever not? Crow said. He's a comely lad.

Just use it for the paintings, I said, all right?

Danny! I shouted, let's go!

At the bridge I said to Danny: Take the wheel mate, will you?

The faces of John Rose, Michael, Stella and Danny, monumental, permanent, looked down at us.

How do you like being on the bridge, Danny? Laurel said.

It's fucking brilliant, Danny said.

Glanced at me, then back to the wheel. Expertly holding us before the bridge.

Water stains made fantastic shapes on the paintings. Bird shit dripping down. Big dollop on John's face. The paintings were already sun-faded and blistered.

On clear days the big faces reflected the river, and seemed to be alive with movement. Kids climbing down from the bridge or hanging over the edge had tagged them with marker pen and spray-paint graffiti. Stickers, burn marks from who knew what, unknown smears on John's black hat.

They looked even better than I'd hoped.

Like they'd always been there.

We did say, did we not, Terry . . . Crow began.

I didn't listen to the rest of it, Crow praising me and the girl agreeing how wonderful I was. Crow was into the paintings, that's what mattered.

Fetched out my flask from where I'd stashed it in the bow.

This is excellent coffee Terry, Crow said. You do very well for yourself here.

You really think we could make money from all this? I said.

Crow looked at me hard.

You do understand I've always been thinking ahead Terry, he said. On your behalf. I want you to remember that.

I get it, I said. You've explained it.

We should start with a film, Laurel said. People see that, they'll want to come and look for themselves. There are multiple ways to monetize that, as my godfather understood.

Smart, lovely to look at, but iron-hard.

What are you thinking? I said.

Well, Laurel said, a gift shop for starters. You'd need to establish ownership of the paintings and reproduction rights. I could look into it for you, she said, and smiled a brilliant smile.

Crow was smiling too. He looked up at the faces on the bridge, and spread his arms as though embracing them. Like a man whose horse has come in. The outside bet.

There are historical precedents, he said. This could really blow up into something big.

Does this mean you're gonna be rich? Danny said.

When we got back I had to remind Crow to give the boy the tenner we'd agreed on.

I piloted the Zodiac towards the line of draping willows on the far side of the river. The water and the trees, the vertical lawns and Spanish tiled roofs of the big houses were all coming in violet as the sun disappeared.

The tide running inland from the sea. Water levels rising.

Cold air edged the river funk into hard shapes.

Felt naked without Red in the boat, her muzzle resting on the inflatable bow, watching the standing finger waves race.

Fallen leaves made patterns on the water, turned in circles, drifted, carried on the tide. The fall of leaves still new enough to notice. Slow flames on the water. Running colour.

Looked back the way I'd come. The high trees made the island a dark shape, pinned with weak and low lights. Hoped Red was all right. I'd cleaned up the boat and fed her before coming back out. Made a lead and collar out of a boat rope and my belt and took her into the forest. When I didn't let her go she looked at me like she wanted to rip my throat out. Locked her in before I left.

Could hear John saying: There's people around here will shoot a strange dog on sight.

Darker now. Violet to purple to dark chocolate. Cut the

engine so that I was drifting on water through trailing willow branches. Among the trees where it was darker still. Turned on the torch. Turned the wheel to follow the path the torch made on the water. Eyeshine of frogs bright scattered points in the torchlight. Then I was through the willows, and into a lighter clearing.

Kaplan's cruiser looked too big for the dock. The gleaming boat was cradled and illuminated by lights set into the pilings. At the waterline, water was reflected on the hull as dancing lighted tracers. In the water leaves crowded the boat and stuck to her hull. The upper deck and bridge were all in darkness, with only irregular glims flashing from the chrome and glass as the boat dipped and rose gently on the river.

Kaplan was waiting on the dock. Behind him the huge lawn led up to the large, castellated house. Starbursts of light from the windows illuminated in patches the gravel path that fringed the house.

It's very good indeed to meet you at last, he said.

Threw Kaplan the rope. He caught it with a fluid movement and tied off the dinghy.

I'll meet you there, Crow had said. I have a car on the mainland. Chance to have a talk with Alex before you arrive.

Kaplan's white shirt gleamed in the light-split darkness. A line of shiny buttons described a swell over his rooster chest. Shorter than me. Standing square on. Legs indistinct, but he was bigger above the waist.

Come along, he said. They're waiting for us.

Kaplan's phone buzzed constantly but he never looked at it.

Kaplan took me into the room where I had brought John Rose, though it was not sunlit now. It was artificial lamplight that made the dark hardwood floor shine. The vases were filled with new stargazer lilies. The same side table of bottled spirits, the levels of alcohol fallen since I had been there last.

Evelyn Crow was standing by the empty fireplace.

There was a chair near the drinks table. A red-haired woman – a thicker, older version of Alexandra – sat on the chair near the mantelpiece with a heavy-looking engraved glass in her hand, half full or half empty of a liquid so clear it was almost blue. Behind her thick make-up she had a faraway look like she'd forgotten something. Maybe in another room, or in another house in another town, long ago.

You know Sir Evelyn of course, Kaplan said. And this is my wife Marina.

Kaplan's wife was trying not to be annoyed by my boots tracking dirt and river water across the hard boards of her floor. I could smell damp and woodsmoke in my clothes, though my sweatshirt and work trousers were the cleanest I could find. I walked over to greet her. Moving stiffly like a monster. Pain recently returned. My stained hands pushing down on the back of a studded leather armchair for support.

Marina poured herself another drink.

The painter, she said, pronouncing each word carefully.

In whose honour we are gathered.

Shall I call Alexandra, dear? Kaplan said. You look tired.

Neither of us have the slightest idea where our daughter is, Marina Kaplan said. Staying out all hours, talking back to her mother. Running around with boys from the island doing God knows what. You should be out looking for her.

I have to talk to these men Marina, Kaplan said.

I'm not stopping you, she said, and held out her glass to Evelyn Crow. If it's more important than the safety of our only child.

She looked up at Crow.

Would you be so kind? she said.

Crow did the honours. Handed me a glass of red wine. A big one.

Hello Terry, he said.

I held the glass but didn't drink.

Laurel not here? I said.

Gone back to town, Crow said. Laurel Archer has great plans for you Terry, great plans.

I'm a developer Terry, Kaplan said. As I'm sure you know. The last few years I've been working with local councils to regenerate neglected housing estates and surrounding neighbourhoods. With some success I must say. I've used some of that success to invest in art and artists.

My husband's interest in art is limited to the kind he can sell for more money than he paid for it, Marina said.

Sir Evelyn bought you to my attention some time ago, Kaplan said.

News to me.

I'll be honest, he said, when I heard that you had moved

here and were working I was more than interested. The unpleasantness over my changes to the island was largely expected. But this business of the pictures was something else. To be frank, I see an opportunity.

A slick operation. Local councils neglected their housing estates and high-rises and the people who lived there. Refused to invest then blamed the tenants. Developers come in and determine the estate is beyond saving. Demolished. People are relocated to unknown neighbourhoods, dormitory accommodation, hostels, single rooms in shit hotels, sometimes even to distant towns. New buildings go up. Much improved. Rents increased as a result, original tenants can't return. People with more money move in. People kicked out rot away out of sight. Developer gets richer.

An opportunity? I said.

Yes, Kaplan said. For the pictures to become the face of the regeneration project. To give it credibility. Something a little different to attract investors and settlers. There are half a dozen islands along this stretch of river. I own them all. We're going to build houses, marinas, wave pools, businesses. Transform them.

You want to use my pictures to hide the fact that you're driving people out of their homes? I said.

You sound like my daughter, Marina said.

She had been still and quiet and I thought she had fallen asleep. The glass Crow had filled for her was empty. I hadn't touched mine.

You should have let her talk to the police, she said. You ruined her Alex. You ruined my baby. You and that dirty boy.

She began to cry silently.

Kaplan, with no expression on his face, briefly put his hand on his wife's shoulder.

I'd like to show you something Terry, he said.

Crow and I followed Kaplan out of the room. Nobody said anything to his wife.

Kaplan's heels struck against the shining floorboards and the reflected sound was loud in the house.

The light in the picture-lined corridor he steered me down made his hair seem blue. My boots thumped against the floor but made no echo.

A large room full of paintings.

A picture window looked out onto the lawn and down to the dock with its muted lights. The brightness in the room crushed my ability to see anything beyond the dock. The island and our settlement of boats did not exist.

The room smelled of stale cigar smoke and strong spirits. There was a thick, half-smoked cigar in a glass ashtray on a round table. The table was crowded with framed photos of Kaplan with military men and, I guessed, important politicians or businessmen, none I recognized.

There was a framed series of drawings by Burke Damis on the far wall. Sketches for the famous Colombian series. The carnival at Barranquilla.

There was also a small drawing by Ariel Galton. A floating grid, rough gold and coral pastels in a sequence that seemed random but was not. The drawing annotated with pencil-written numbers I knew to be measurements. Worked up, the finished painting would be huge. I'd never seen it, but I imagined the painting as light held in space, the colours alive and pulsing. Transmitting blasts of pure emotion.

Sir Evelyn says you're an admirer, Kaplan said.

She was the only real painter we've had in years, I said.

Terry, Crow said.

Filling the wall behind me was one of my pictures. The show that never was. The painting of the group of ex-miners I'd met on a beach in Kent. Watching two of their number fighting. Bare-chested in the cold. Pastels. Red submerged under white skin. A sand-blown car park. Ice cream vans parked for the winter. Split colour field. Grey overcast sky, ochre ground. Watchers in black clothes.

Seven men, all told. None had worked since the pits closed. After the strike. In the end they were too old to work. Too old to fight, but it was an honour match. One man was revealed as a scab.

The seven men had walked to the car park from the union club where they came, separately and together, once a fortnight to drink the subsidized beer. A bitter wind came off the grey sea, but the fighters took off their old suit jackets and clean shirts to settle their business for the same reason they had all left the warm and neat union club.

The strike had been over for more than thirty years. If you didn't have your good name what did you have? Lost everything else. The alleged strike-breaker was a stranger in the area who believed his history was unknown. Passed himself off as a good man. Long time ago but not long enough. Recognized. The accused man told to choose an opponent. Chose his accuser.

Bodies ghostly pale, somehow glaring on a sunless day. Marked by jagged sawtooth scars. Work injuries visible on the clothed men as missing fingers, one shoulder held lower than the other. The wind whipping paper rubbish off the tarmac. A fist smacking against cold flesh at too long intervals. Heavy breaths. Gasping and finite. The watching men stone-faced under caps. Silent. Duty. Take no pleasure.

The scab was put down by weakly thrown punches that had been travelling for decades. Six men left the beaten one alone on the ground. Back to their pints and songs in the union club. A small, unknown museum decorated with the faded honours of the past.

The picture reminds me of my father, Kaplan said.

I don't see how, I said.

My father fought for everything he had. Said we had to break the power of the unions to get free. You had to go after the toughest. The miners, the printers. Agreed with Thatcher. Winning the miners' strike was the moment we got our country back.

Wasn't worth having back by then, I said.

Terry, Evelyn Crow said.

Nobody does anything unless it's for profit, Kaplan said.

Kaplan wrote something on a piece of paper. Handed it to me.

I put down my still-full glass. Looked at the amount. Looked at Crow.

We can talk about the numbers, Crow said.

I want you to sell me the paintings Terry, Kaplan said.

They're not mine to sell.

Kaplan laughed.

You were right, Kaplan said to Crow. The famous pride.

I think what Terry means, Crow said, is that the pictures belong to the people. Terry would have to get their agreement.

No, I said, you're wrong. The paintings have been given to a charitable trust. I don't have any say in what happens to them. If you want to buy the paintings, Mr Kaplan, you'll have to negotiate with the trust.

What damn trust?

Kaplan's friendliness was gone, evaporated like the alcohol in his wife's glass.

You told me he was coming here to sell me the pictures, he said to Crow. You told me it would be straightforward.

Straightforward the way you got this? I said, looking at my painting.

Who runs this trust? Crow said.

Nancy Rose.

That's a name unknown to me, Terry.

She's John Rose's daughter.

Crow looked blank.

I've never heard of him, Kaplan said.

You just offered me a lot of money for his picture, I said.

The old man on the bridge, Crow said.

John Rose died in this house, I said. Alexandra helped me try to save him. She was brave. I liked her.

Kaplan glared at me. Something of what he felt for his daughter flared up and was visible and dangerous.

Alex told me all about it, he said.

Nancy is more than happy to deal with you, I said to Kaplan, provided certain guarantees and conditions are met.

What kind of guarantees? Kaplan said.

No mooring fee increase for boats that have been here over two years. Investment. A day care centre. Somewhere for the kids to go. Nancy's got a list.

I'll bloody well take them down, Kaplan said.

That would be a bad idea, I said. The paintings are not on your land. The bridge and the weir belong to the council.

What's in it for you? Kaplan said. What are you, sixty? You have no money. You'll become like these men. Fighting in an empty car park.

Some things are more important, I said.

Terry, Crow said.

You dirty bastard, Kaplan said.

Now Alex, Crow said, take a moment. Just consider, if we do this right it could be very good for you. Laurel Archer's film could do wonders.

Crow gestured towards the painting of the miners.

The value of Mr Godden's work, he said, might sharply increase. In fact I'd say it was highly likely.

Marina appeared at the open door. In the light of the hallway, I could see the grey in her red hair.

There's somebody outside, she said.

You're drunk, Kaplan said.

Said my goodbyes. Kaplan said his through a closed mouth. Marina followed us to the door, bumping into walls and furniture as though she had woken up in a strange house. When I left she was standing in the lighted porch, staring into the dark. I walked across the midnight lawn, the border plants and flowers making soft black cut outs. There was nobody out there.

Some things are more important. Who did I think I was, John Wayne? Didn't matter. Looked forward to calling Nancy Rose. Crow was in. Could see himself getting paid. Would sweet-talk Kaplan because it was required. It might work.

Down the steep lawn from the house to the river, I could smell as though for the first time the air that I'd been breathing for over a year. River air. Familiar now. Soaked earth that was never dry, so that the heavy dampness felt ancient. Sometimes so thick and close I could taste it in my mouth and nose, like having earth shovelled onto my face. As I came near the dock some sharpness I couldn't name at first cut into the dampness.

The dock was wet though there had been no rain. Kaplan's big cruiser, bow forwards and tied alongside, glistened. Stepped onto the dock, my boots echoing. Bent and put my fingers to the wood. Water sounded hollowly against the hull of the cruiser and more deeply against the pilings. Everything was soaked in petrol.

I stepped down into the Zodiac and began untying her from the dock piling. The rope was slick in my hands. There was petrol on the water.

The tender began to rock so that I had to sit down on the transom. River water came towards me in a low terraced swell. I heard the engine before I saw Gene, at the bridge of his restored boat, coming out of the gloom. No lights running. Nameless and unpainted, a half-seen ghost of a boat.

Whatever engine he'd salvaged from God knows where idled with a soft churning hum.

Terry, Gene called softly.

Face smeared with dirt and black grease.

Gene, I said.

Saw the tender, he said. Been waiting.

What are you doing here?

Where's the dog? Gene said. Where's old Red?

You selling us out Terry?

Gene, I said, we won Gene. Don't do this. You don't know. We won.

You must be back on the piss Terry, Gene said, you believe that.

Alexandra appeared alongside Gene and passed him a kid's bow and arrow set. The girl's red hair was crushed under a dark cap.

What's she doing here? I said.

I'm here because I want to be, Alexandra said.

She's just a kid Gene, I said.

I can speak for myself, she said.

This won't help you, I said.

How could you possibly know what will help me? she said.

I've lived longer than you, I said.

You know why Michael really died? she said. Because he could only measure his worth against all this.

What John Rose had said when he first told me about the mooring fee increase: I reject the measure by which I am found wanting.

Get your boat moving Terry, Gene said.

I put my hand on the Zodiac's inflated bow, put my hand to my nose.

It all burns the same, Gene said. Whichever side you're on.

He had an arrow fitted to his bow, the head of the arrow bulky with some kind of wrapping.

You're going to fuck everything up Gene.

Everything's already fucked up, he said. They won't send divers. Won't spend the money. Say it's not a priority. Spend the fucking money when they thought I killed him. Michael never mattered.

Michael's not forgotten Gene, I said, he's up on the bridge.

Underwater, Gene said. You painted him underwater.

Gene, I said.

I'm not going to tell you again, Gene said, and raised the bow.

I backed the boat away.

Gene nodded at Alexandra and she lit the end of the arrow with a lighter. The arrowhead flared into flame.

Gene there's fuel in the boat.

I should fucking hope so, he said.

Doors crashing open and more lights going on in

Kaplan's house. Kaplan and Crow appeared at the top of the violet lawn.

Who's out there? Kaplan shouted. That the fucking painter?

Terry! Crow shouted. Terry!

Gene winked at me as he raised the stave of the bow higher.

Fired. The flaming arrow made a fiery arc in the night sky. Lighting up the darkness. The arrow missed the cruiser and landed on the dock and the dock began to burn. Alexandra lit another arrow and Gene raised the bow and fired again. I could hear him laughing. There was a popping sound and the cruiser burst into flames.

I looked away. Pointed the Zodiac into the headwind.

Made for the island with everything behind me on fire, the faint sound of sirens becoming stronger in the distance.

The boats and watching islanders were cast in reflected fire. Burning fragments of boat and wooden pier swirled and drifted across the river, dissolving in mid-air or falling harmlessly onto me, into the boat, the water. The fire did not reach as far as our side of the river, though the sparks kept falling as I came alongside *Vesna*.

I saw Danny and Stella, watching, lit up by the blaze, but they didn't see me.

Anthony Waters held Perseis close. Maybe he heard the tender, I don't know, but he turned and saw me. We stared at each other, until Waters broke the gaze and turned back around. Perseis never knew I was there. Poor kid, I thought, good luck to her.

I went aboard.

Red was gone.

The cabin door forced open. All over the boat, more drops of blood that was not blood. I grabbed a torch and the makeshift rope lead and went out the door, shouting her name. The river was all violet and magenta. Kaplan's dock and cruiser still burned fiercely. Great clouds of charcoal smoke churned upwards. Massive blood-orange flames were reflected in the sky. The air tasted of burning diesel. More sirens sounded from the mainland.

A long way downstream I could see the faint blue light

of a police launch moving fast in midwater. They'd be here soon, and coming onto the island with more cops and security guards and anybody else Kaplan could wake up and get out of bed. Even McNab and Hatchet Face. He'd send everybody to the island. All looking for me. They wouldn't believe I had nothing to do with it. I had to find Red before they came.

I followed her trail into the forest. Under torchlight the red marks were black. The dragging weight of my body, all the dark surround, seemed to fall away. I lost the trail or the trail stopped. Ahead of me was the work site. Dogs barking. There was a radio or a phone playing tinny music. Night security.

The two huge German shepherds barked and snapped their jaws and jumped at the fence. Not chained, but running free inside.

There were dark stains on the fur of both of them. A long handled chisel was jammed between the gate handles either side of the lock mechanism. The gate may have been locked, but there was no padlock I could see. There were small dips and scooped-out places on the ground by the fence where the dogs had been digging. Two men in cheap black uniforms sat in the hut. The guards. Big and Not So Big. The chairs and a small table were the only furniture I could see.

Seen my dog? I shouted, my hands on the fence.

I shook the fence. The bigger of the two men took his feet off the table and stood up. Moved stiffly, like he was hurt somewhere. Said something to his partner. Faces lit up by the sodium-yellow light.

I moved away from the fence. The smaller man shouted at the dogs and eventually they stopped barking. I pointed at the German shepherds, one prowling along the fence line, one sat on the ground mouthing and licking at something that seemed caught in its fur. Both bitches, but big dogs, with huge heads and thick paws.

I pointed at the dogs and pointed at me.

My dog, I said, have you seen her?

The big man shook his head, and pointed into the forest. The not-so-big guard said something in a rushed voice, and the big man said something hard and fast that shut him up. The other man took something lead coloured and threw it to the corner of the room so that it landed heavily.

I went back into the forest. Michael's stones. I switched off the torch. Silver-edged ceramic hearts span slowly in the trees. Wind chimes and dream catchers. I stood surrounded by kids' pictures. Many had Red in them. Easy to pick out because of her brightness. Red running in the forest. Inside a ring of children. Swimming in the river. Always at the heart of things. Sometimes a white-faced man in dark clothes is with her. In one he has his arms around the dog, and is smiling.

John Rose had carved a rough picture of Red on the wood of an old fruit box and put it in a tree. Cheap wood, light as balsa, with that almost honey colour, and in the darkness of the forest Red's picture was a source, something precious, giving off a kind of magic-hour light.

I kept calling Red's name, quieter each time, then I stopped. I figured I'd gone far enough to convince the men in the hut. The German shepherds had been wet around the mouth. Their fur was stained with something dark. No padlock on the gate.

There was an iron skip filled with rubbish, building materials, supply bags, rubble from the cleared ground.

I found her hidden behind some plasterboard discards. She was stuffed inside a bag that had been full of cement. When I lifted her out of the bag she was covered with strange pearl-like beads made from the grey cement thickening with her blood. I laid her on the ground. Around her throat there were strings of these red-grey beads, and many more down the centre of her where she had been ripped open. Her lips were drawn back from her teeth and her mouth was open, like when she was asleep and dreaming, but she would not dream any more. I lifted her paws, saw the broken nails wet with blood. The brave light in her eye was gone for the first time.

I kneeled before her. I put my hands in her fur and rubbed it against the grain like I had the first time I'd seen her, and she had been no bigger than my hand. She was already cold. I picked her off the ground and cradled her. I buried my face in her fur and then I laid her back down. I kissed her.

Wait there, sweetheart.

I doubled back, making a big loop through the trees to come out behind the work site and the security guards' hut.

The moon was up, and followed me between the tall

dark trees. Walked softly, holding the rope and belt so that they did not drag on the ground. Sodium-yellow light showed in a small back window. Also a door.

I weighed the cold belt buckle in my hands. Wrapped the end of the rope around my left hand, making a hard pad, and tied it off. The rest of the rope hung whitely, weighted by the leather belt and hard buckle.

I made a low run to the door. Reached for the handle with my right hand. Felt the handle give as I pulled it slowly downwards. I let it back up. I stood, holding the length of rope in my bound hand. Yanked the door open and went in.

The big man was talking into the radio. The other man was smoking a cigarette and listening. The music I'd heard had stopped.

All right, the man said. All right. Just left. No, on his own. You want us to go after him? No, on his own, I told you. Nothing else we could do. What's going on up there?

The big man looked up.

Wait, he said, Mr Kaplan, he's here . . .

I ran at the big man, fast, as if he were a door closing, speeding up as I reached him.

The big man was still rising from his chair when I smashed him in the face with my rope thickened fist. He crashed to the floor. The dogs were at the window, jumping up in a frenzy, jaws open, thick lengths of saliva streaking the glass, claws scratching on the cheap wood. The other man stood with his hands raised. I lashed him with the rope.

The big man rose and I hit him again with the rope and

buckle. The buckle split his face open and he screamed and fell.

I went back to the other man and started to hit him and he put his hands up. The big guard spat something onto the floor.

Fucking kill you, he said. Fucking mutt.

Stay down, I said.

Threw the radio on the floor and stamped on it until it broke apart.

All the time the shepherds going mad.

Left the hut. Cops and guards were coming. I could hear them shouting, crashing through the forest, beams of torch-light moving wildly between the dark trees.

The dock still burned. Way downstream I could see the bridge, returned once more to abstract forms, my paintings disappeared.

Went back to my dog. Kneeled and kissed her again.

Good soldier, I said, and then I lifted her up and carried her away into the forest.

Good soldier.

Author's Note

In late December 2016, I went with my wife to see Slovakian artist Roman Ondak's show at the South London Gallery. Despite living for thirty years no more than a few minutes away from the gallery on Peckham Road in Camberwell, I'd never been there before. I can't explain this, as I was in the habit of visiting one of London's free galleries at least once a week. Except to walk my dog, this was also the first time I'd left the house since my mother's funeral two months earlier.

Beneath the floor of the gallery is a marquetry panel designed by the nineteenth-century artist, designer and socialist Walter Crane (1845–1915). Commissioned as a centrepiece for the gallery, which opened in 1891, it's believed to be the only piece of its kind that Crane made.

Most often hidden from view, Ondak uncovered Crane's floor for the first time in many years, as part of his installation. The timing was right.

It was dark outside. From its place on the floor the panel seemed to float up, and become suspended in the centre of an otherwise overwhelmingly white space (which was not white, I'm sure, in the radiant way I experienced it). Swans, bulrushes and shells, diamond and fish-scale patterns rose before me.

I was open to visions and instruction. Both devastated,

as Roland Barthes wrote eight days after his mother's death, and the victim of presence of mind. The colours of the inlaid wood, the patterns, the shells and bulrushes, the *brownness*, all of this reminded me of my grandad Jim, a Dunkirk veteran, and nan Millie. In the late 1960s when I was a really little kid, they'd been moved from their small house in the centre of Eastbourne to a tiny flat on the eastern edge of the town. The house and street – where I spent the first four years of my life – was demolished to make way for a multi-storey car park.

Crane's panel reminded me of Nan's brown furniture – her inherited dark sideboard and fold-out table, her fire screen, all so beautifully and carefully made. I remembered how Nan – my mum's mum – took great care of these things that had once belonged to her father, Charles Lawrence, a train driver, Methodist lay preacher and Labour councillor.

At the centre of Crane's panel is the inscription: The Source of Art is in the Life of a People.

Sometimes only the obvious will do – the words hit me like a punch, a command and a question, or series of questions. What art? What people? What is the relationship of the people to the art once the art is made? Are the people from whose lives the art is made the same people that consume, own or otherwise benefit from the finished work? What are the responsibilities of the artist who accepts Crane's challenge? What is the relationship of the artist to the people? If the artist makes art from the lives of the people, are there certain kinds of art that can and cannot be made?

The Painter's Friend is the result of working through these questions, as well as being an exploration of what it means and has meant to be a working class artist in a country where, as B. S. Johnson wrote in *Trawl* (1964), a novel published the year I was born: 'The class war is being fought as viciously and destructively of human spirit as it ever has been in England: I was born on my side, and I cannot and will not desert.'

The Painter's Friend is indebted to Mark Aitken's award-winning photography project *Sanctum Ephemeral*, a series of portraits made inside homes in Cressingham Gardens, a south London housing estate threatened with demolition. Aitken's decision to install the photographs as large prints on the estate's exterior walls inspires Terry's actions. Thanks to Mark for his counsel and blessing. Lines from Mark's emails to me have been used, in slightly different form, on p. 171.

See also Mark Aitken, *Sanctum Ephemeral* (Deep River Press, 2018), with a short text, 'Nothing Here Before' (pp. 38–9) by Howard Cunnell and afterword by Zelda Cheatle.

This book is dedicated to the writer John Healy. Terry Godden's expulsion from the art industry deliberately invokes Healy's treatment at the hands of the UK publishing industry after his classic memoir, *The Grass Arena*, was published by Faber in 1988.

Healy's book became a prize-winning bestseller, but after the writer had allegedly made threats of physical violence against publishing staff, *The Grass Arena* was withdrawn from sale. Copies were pulped and the book was put out of print.

Healy's work was then effectively suppressed for years, depriving the writer of an income. In 2019, Etruscan Books published *The Metal Mountain*, the writer's first novel in thirty years. John Healy has never stopped writing.

Burke Damis is the pseudonym of the painter Bruce Campion in Ross Macdonald's novel *The Zebra Striped Hearse* (1962). Laurel Archer is named both for the character Laurel Russo in *Sleeping Beauty* (1973), and for Lew Archer, Macdonald's private detective. Ariel Galton's surname is taken from Macdonald's *The Galton Case* (1959).

Island, a short story in which the people who will become Gene, Perseis and Michael first appeared, was published by Pariah Press in 2015.

Lines from p. 29 were first published in slightly different form in my poem 'Near Bells Yew Green', in Michael Curran (ed.), *Scare-Devil* (Sick Fly Publications / Tangerine Press. Tooting, 2019), p. 23.

Lines from pp. 28, 50 and 51 were first published in slightly different form in my poem 'Some Way off the Island', in

Michael Curran (ed.), *Fool-Saint* (Sick Fly Publications/Tangerine Press. Tooting, 2020), pp. 16–17.

p. 61: 'All bones, breath and eyes, Vesna. So thin the joints showed through.'
Gary Snyder, 'Go Now', in *The Present Moment: New Poems* (Counterpoint. Berkeley, 2015), p. 63: 'So thin that the joints showed through / each sinew and knob . . . her / lips dry, fierce, she was all bones, breath and eyes'.

p. 97: 'When will I be done keeping this fist clenched in my chest my throat my skull?'
George Mouratidis, 'Gentry Street Saturday 4 p.m. Greens' (or 'Notes While Waiting for Laundry'), in *Angel Frankenstein* (Soulbay Press. Sydney, 2018), p. 104. Thanks to George Mouratidis.

p. 131: 'I thought of ships, of armies, hanging on.'
Charles Bukowski, 'I Thought of Ships, of Armies, Hanging On', in *The Days Run Away Like Wild Horses Over the Hills* (Black Sparrow Press. Santa Rosa, 1969), p. 63: 'and I thought of ships, of armies / hanging on'.

p. 205: 'Making money with the sun on their backs, dreaming of a beach-bar getaway.'
Mick Guffan, 'Workers Dream of a Beach Bar Getaway', in *Inner London Buddha: Selected Poems 1999–2006* (Tangerine Press. Tooting, 2018), p. 110: 'But there / will be workers

dreaming / of a beach bar getaway / at a negligent corner / of an impossible town'. Thanks to Michael Curran.

p. 227: 'It's become a kind of urban myth.'

In an interview for the documentary film *Barbaric Genius* (2001), former Faber Editor-in-Chief Robert McCrum described the row with writer John Healy, after which *The Grass Arena* was pulped and put out of print, as 'insignificant' and a kind of 'urban myth'.

Acknowledgements

My love and thanks to the following for their contributions to this book: Mark Aitken Adjoa Andoh Irene Babinet Paul Baggaley Sean Baker Frank Bowling John Bratby Anne Briggs Charles Bukowski Edward Burra Joyce Cary Joseph Conrad Rob Coyne Wendy Coyne Walter Crane Rebecca Crow Gillian Cunnell (née Godden) Mark Cunnell Michael Curran Sandy Denny Kris Doyle Andrew Franks Marcus Harvey Ted Giles Brian Godden James Godden Jo Godden Mary Godden Millie Godden (née Lawrence) Davy Graham Debra Granik Valeska Grisebach Melissa Harrison John Healy Samantha Herron Violet Hodsall (née Lawrence) John Hoyland Mark Jenkin Tom Jenkins Keith King Sophie Lambert Charles Lawrence Cyril Lawrence Matthew Loukes Jim MacAirt Ross Macdonald Jock McFadyen Adam Mars-Jones Agnes Martin Rowan Moore Van Morrison George Mouratidis Les Murray Sophie Newell Robert Noonan Roman Ondak Jonathan Rendall David Rogers James Sallis George Shaw Gary Snyder Alan Stepney Beverley Toogood Alex Trocchi Patrick Walsh Adele Waters Steve Waters Roy Williams Tim Winton

Love to the dogs: Angel Boy Edward Fordie Hattie India Lulu Millie Rosa Sparkle Tally